"What do I get if I find your nephew's team a coach?"

Lucy wondered if Ryland was serious or teasing her. His smile suggested the latter. "My undying gratitude?"

"That's a good start."

"More cookies?"

"Always appreciated—especially if they're chocolate chip, which happen to be my favorite," he said. "What else?"

His light-hearted and flirty tone sounded warning bells in her head. Ryland *was* teasing her, but Lucy no longer wanted to play along. His charm, pretty much everything about him, left her…unsettled. "I'm not sure what else you might want."

He gave her the once-over, only this time his gaze lingered a second too long on her lips. "I can think of a couple things."

Dear Reader

For the past eight years my fall and spring Dedication Weekends have been full of soccer games. I don't see this ending any time soon. My oldest daughter has stopped playing, but my other two children still play. And my husband has coached recreational teams for the past six years.

Soccer isn't something I grew up with. I attended my first game in 1984, but wasn't really sure what was going on. And I was on a soccer team with co-workers, but I joined that more to meet people than play the game. Friends kept telling me how big soccer—they called it football—was outside the US, but I never realised how big until June 26th 1994, when I attended a World Cup match between Colombia and Switzerland at Stanford Stadium. Not even the two Super Bowls I'd gone to came close to matching the excitement and passion of these soccer fans.

Ever since then I've wanted to write a romance with soccer as the background, but it wasn't until my son started playing competitive soccer for an Oregon club in spring 2010 that the story ideas started flowing. You see, one of my son's coaches also played for the Portland Timbers—this was the year before they became a Major League soccer team. After speaking with him my hero, a professional soccer player named Ryland James, came to life.

Having access to people who can help with research adds realism to a story—though I usually take some artistic licence for plot purposes. I was fortunate in the soccer assistance I received, but when it came to my heroine Lucy, who'd had a liver transplant as a teen, I wasn't sure where to turn for help.

A friend had been a living donor for her daughter's successful liver transplant in 2007, but I happened to mention my work-in-progress to another mom, Bernice Conrad, during our kids' swimming practice. Turned out Bernice was a two-time liver and kidney transplant recipient. Talking with her helped me understand and fill in Lucy's backstory of her having liver failure. It also made me understand the importance of organ donation and the lives being saved by transplants.

To all those who have signed up to be donors: thank you!

Melissa

IT STARTED WITH
A CRUSH...

BY
MELISSA McCLONE

First published in Great Britain 2010
by Mills & Boon, an imprint of Harlequin (UK) Limited,
Eton House, 18-24 Paradise Road, Richmond, Surrey TW9 1SR

© Melissa Martinez McClone 2012

ISBN: 978 0 263 22741 3

cwable
tainable
the

With a degree in mechanical engineering from Stanford University, the last thing **Melissa McClone** ever thought she would be doing was writing romance novels. But analysing engines for a major US airline just couldn't compete with her 'happily-ever-afters'. When she isn't writing, caring for her three young children or doing laundry, Melissa loves to curl up on the couch with a cup of tea, her cats and a good book. She enjoys watching home decorating shows to get ideas for her house—a 1939 cottage that is *slowly* being renovated. Melissa lives in Lake Oswego, Oregon, with her own real-life hero husband, two daughters, a son, two loveable but oh-so-spoiled indoor cats and a no-longer-stray outdoor kitty that decided to call the garage home.

Melissa loves to her from her readers. You can write to her at PO Box 63, Lake Oswego, OR 97034, USA, or contact her via her website: www.melissamcclone.com

Recent titles by the same author:

FIREFIGHTER UNDER THE MISTLETOE
EXPECTING ROYAL TWINS!
NOT-SO-PERFECT PRINCESS

**Did you know these are also available as eBooks?
Visit www.millsandboon.co.uk**

For all the people who generously volunteer their time to coach kids—especially those who have made such a difference in my children's lives. Thank you!

Special thanks to: Josh Cameron, Brian Verrinder, Ian Burgess, Bernice Conrad and Terri Reed.

CHAPTER ONE

EVERY day for the past four weeks, Connor's school bus had arrived at the corner across the street no later than three-thirty. Every day, except today. Lucy Martin glanced at the clock hanging on the living-room wall.

3:47 p.m.

Anxiety knotted her stomach making her feel jittery. Her nephew should be home by now.

Was it time to call the school to find out where the bus might be or was she overreacting? This parenting—okay, surrogate parenting—thing was too new to know for certain.

She stared out the window, hoping the bus would appear. The street corner remained empty. That wasn't surprising. Only residents drove through this neighborhood on the outskirts of town.

What to do? She tapped her foot.

Most contingencies and emergencies had been listed in the three-ring binder Lucy called the survival guide. Her sister-in-law, Dana, had put it together before she left. But a late school bus hadn't been one of the scenarios. Lucy had checked. Twice.

No need to panic. Wicksburg was surrounded by farmland, a small town with a low crime rate and zero excitement except for harvests in the summer, Friday-night football games in the fall and basketball games in the winter. A number of things could have delayed the bus. A traffic jam due to slow-moving farm equipment, road construction, a car accident...

A chill shivered down Lucy's spine.

Don't freak out. Okay, she wasn't used to taking care of anyone but herself. This overwhelming need to see her nephew right this moment was brand-new to her. But she'd better get used to it. For the next year she wasn't only Connor's aunt, she was also his guardian while his parents, both army reservists, were deployed overseas. Her older brother, Aaron, was counting on Lucy to take care of his only child. If something happened to Connor on her watch...

Her muscles tensed.

"Meow."

The family's cat, an overweight Maine Coon with a tail that looked more like a raccoon's than a feline's, rubbed against the front door. His green-eyed gaze met Lucy's.

"I know, Manny." The cat's concern matched her own. "I want Connor home, too."

Something caught the corner of her eye. Something yellow. She stared out the window once again.

The school bus idled at the corner. Red lights flashed.

Relief flowed through her. "Thank goodness."

Lucy took a step toward the front door then stopped. Connor had asked her not to meet him at the bus stop. She understood the need to be independent and wanted to make him happy. But not even following his request these past two and a half weeks had erased the sadness from his eyes. She knew better than to take it personally. Smiles had become rare commodities around here since his parents deployed.

Peering through the slit in the curtains gave her a clear view of the bus and the short walk to the house. Connor could assert his independence while she made sure he was safe.

Lucy hated seeing him moping around like a lost puppy, but she understood. He missed his parents. She'd tried to make him feel better. Nothing, not even his favorite desserts, fast-food restaurants or video games, had made a difference. Now that his spring soccer team was without a coach, things had gone from bad to worse.

The door of the bus opened. The Bowman twins exited. The

seven-year-old girls wore matching pink polka-dot dresses, white shoes and purple backpacks.

Connor stood on the bus's bottom step with a huge smile on his face. He leaped to the ground and skipped away.

Her heart swelled with excitement. Something good must have happened at school.

As her nephew approached the house, Lucy stepped away from the window. She wanted to make sure his smile remained. No matter what it took.

Manny rubbed against her leg. Birdlike chirping sounds came from his mouth. Strange, but not unexpected from a cat that barked when annoyed.

"Don't worry, Manny." She touched the cat's back. "Connor will be home in three...two...one..."

The front door flung open. Manny dashed for the outside, but Connor closed the door to stop his escape.

"Aunt Lucy." His blue eyes twinkled. So much like Aaron. Same eyes, same hair color, same freckles. "I found someone who can coach the Defeeters."

She should have known Connor's change of attitude had to do with soccer. Her nephew loved the sport. Aaron had coached his son's team, the Defeeters, since Connor started playing organized soccer when he was five. A dad had offered to coach in Aaron's place, but then had to back out after his work schedule changed. No other parent could do it for a variety of reasons. That left the team without a coach. Well, unless you counted her, which was pretty much like being coachless.

The thought of asking her ex-husband to help entered her mind for about a nanosecond before she banished it into the far recesses of her brain where really bad ideas belonged. Being back in the same town as Jeff was hard enough with all the not-so-pleasant memories resurfacing. Lucy hadn't seen him yet nor did she want to.

"Fantastic," she said. "Who is it?"

Connor's grin widened, making him look as if he'd found a million-dollar bill or calorie-free chocolate. He shrugged off his backpack. "Ryland James."

Her heart plummeted to her feet. Splat! "*The* Ryland James?"

Connor nodded enthusiastically. "He's not only best player in the MLS, but my favorite. He'll be the perfect coach. He played on the same team with my dad. They won district and a bunch of tournaments. Ryland's a nice guy. My dad said so."

She had to tread carefully here. For Connor's sake.

Ryland *had* been a nice guy and one of her brother's closest friends. But she hadn't seen him since he left high school to attend the U.S. Soccer Residency Program in Florida. According to Aaron, Ryland had done well, playing overseas and now for the Phoenix Fuego, a Major League Soccer (MLS) team in the U.S. Coaching a recreational soccer team comprised of nine-year-olds probably wasn't on his bucket list.

Lucy bit the inside of her cheek, hoping to think of something—anything—that wouldn't make this blow up in her face and turn Connor's smile upside down.

"Wow," she said finally. "Ryland James would be an amazing coach, but don't you think he's getting ready to start training for his season?"

"MLS teams have been working out in Florida and Arizona since January. The season opener isn't until April." Connor spoke as if this was common knowledge she should know. Given soccer had always been "the sport" in the Martin household, she probably should. "But Ryland James got hurt playing with the U.S. Men's Team in a friendly against Mexico. He's out for a while."

Friendly meant an exhibition game. Lucy knew that much. But the news surprised her. Aaron usually kept her up-to-date on Ryland. Her brother would never let Lucy forget her schoolgirl crush on the boy from the wrong side of town who was now a famous soccer star. "Hurt as in injured?"

"He had surgery and can't play for a couple of months. He's staying with his parents while he recovers." Connor's eyes brightened more. "Isn't that great?"

"I wouldn't call having surgery and being injured great."

"Not him being hurt, but his being in town and able to coach us." Connor made it sound like this was a done deal. "I bet Ryland James will be almost as good a coach as my dad."

"Did someone ask Ryland if he would coach the Defeeters?"

"No," Connor admitted, undaunted. "I came up with the idea during recess after Luke told me Ryland James was at the fire station's spaghetti feed signing autographs. But the whole team thinks it's a good idea. If I'd been there last night..."

The annual Wicksburg Fire Department Spaghetti Feed was one of the biggest events in town. She and Connor had decided not to go to the fundraiser because Dana was calling home. "Don't forget, you got to talk to your mom."

"I know," Connor said. "But I'd like Ryland James's autograph. If he coaches us, he can sign my ball."

Signing a few balls, mugging for the camera and smiling at soccer moms didn't come close to the time it would take to coach a team of boys. The spring season was shorter and more casual than fall league, but still...

She didn't want Connor to be disappointed. "It's a great idea, but Ryland might not have time."

"Will you ask him if he'll coach us, Aunt Lucy? He might just say yes."

The sound of Connor's voice, full of excitement and anticipation, tugged at her heart. "Might" likely equaled "yes" in his young mind. She'd do anything for her nephew. She'd returned to the same town where her ex, now married to her former best friend, lived in order to care for Connor but going to see Ryland...

She blew out a puff of air. "He could say no."

The last time Lucy had seen him had been before her liver transplant. She'd been in eighth grade, jaundiced and bloated, carrying close to a hundred pounds of extra water weight. Not to mention totally exhausted and head over heels in love with the high-school soccer star. She'd spent much of her time alone in her room due to liver failure. Ryland James had fueled her adolescent fantasies. She'd dreamed about him letting her wear his jersey, asking her out to see a movie at the Liberty Theater and inviting her to be his date at prom.

Of course, none of those things had ever happened. She'd hated being known as the sick girl. She'd rarely been able to get up the nerve to say a word to Ryland. And then…

The high-school soccer team had put on two fundraisers—a summer camp for kids and a goal-a-thon—to help with Lucy's medical expenses. She remembered when Ryland handed her the large cardboard check. She'd tried to push her embarrassment and awkwardness aside by smiling at him and meeting his gaze. He'd surprised her by smiling back and sending her heart rate into overdrive. She'd never forgot his kindness or the flash of pity in his eyes. She'd been devastated.

Lucy's stomach churned at the memory. She wasn't that same girl. Still, she didn't want to see him again.

"Ryland is older than me." No one could ever imagine what she'd gone through and how she'd felt being so sick and tired all the time. Or how badly she'd wanted to be normal and healthy. "He was your dad's friend, not mine. I really didn't know him."

"But you've met him."

"He used to come to our house, but the chances of him remembering me…"

"Please, Aunt Lucy." Connor's eyes implored her. "We'll never know unless you ask."

Darn. He sounded like Aaron. Never willing to give up no matter what the odds. Her brother wouldn't let her give up, either. Not when she would have died without a liver transplant or when Jeff had trampled upon her heart.

Lucy's chest tightened. She should do this for Aaron as much as Connor. But she had no idea how she could get close enough to someone as rich and famous as Ryland James.

Connor stared up at her with big, round eyes.

A lump formed in her throat. Whether she wanted to see Ryland James or could see him didn't matter. This wasn't about her. "Okay. I'll ask him."

Connor wrapped his arms around her. "I knew I could count on you."

Lucy hugged him tight. "You can always count on me, kiddo."

Even if she knew going into this things wouldn't work out the way her nephew wanted. But she could keep him smiling a little while longer. At least until Ryland said no.

Connor squirmed out of her arms. "Let's go see him now."

"Not so fast. This is something I'm doing on my own." She didn't want her nephew's image of his favorite soccer player destroyed in case Ryland was no longer a nice guy. Fame or fortune could change people. "And I can't show up empty-handed."

But what could she give to a man who could afford whatever he wanted? Flowers might be appropriate given his injury, but maybe a little too feminine. Chocolate, perhaps? Hershey Kisses might give him the wrong idea. Not that he'd ever known about her crush.

"Cookies," Connor suggested. "Everyone likes cookies."

"Yes, they do." Though Lucy doubted anything would convince Ryland to accept the coaching position. But what was the worst he could say besides no? "Does chocolate chip sound good?"

"Those are my favorite." Connor's smile faltered. "It's too bad my mom isn't here. She makes the best chocolate-chip cookies."

Lucy mussed his hair to keep him from getting too caught up in missing his mom. "It is too bad, but remember she's doing important stuff right now. Like your dad."

Connor nodded.

"How about we use your mom's recipe?" Lucy asked. "You can show me how she makes them."

His smile returned. "Okay."

Lucy wanted to believe everything would turn out okay, but she knew better. As with marriage, the chance of a happy ending here was extremely low. Best to prepare accordingly. She would make a double batch of cookies—one to give to Ryland and one for them to keep. She and Connor were going to need something to make them feel better after Ryland James said no.

* * *

The dog's whimpering almost drowned out the pulse-pounding rock music playing in his parents' home gym.

Ryland didn't glance at Cupcake. The dog could wait. He needed to finish his workout.

Lying on the weight machine's bench, he raised the bar overhead, doing the number of reps recommended by the team's trainer. He used free weights when he trained in Phoenix, but his parents wanted him using the machine when he worked out alone.

Sweat beaded on his forehead. He'd ditched his T-shirt twenty minutes ago. His bare back stuck to the vinyl.

Ryland tightened his grip on the handles.

He wanted to return to the team in top form, to show them he still deserved the captaincy as well as their respect. He'd already lost one major endorsement deal due to his bad-boy behavior. For all he knew, he might not even have a spot on the Fuego roster come opening day. And that...sucked.

On the final rep, his muscles ached and his arms trembled. He clenched his jaw, pushing the weight overhead one last time.

"Yes!"

He'd increased the amount of weight this morning. His trainer would be pleased with the improvements in upper-body strength. That and his core were the only things he could work on.

Ryland sat up, breathing hard. Not good. He needed to keep up his endurance while he healed from the surgery.

Damn foot. He stared at his right leg encased in a black walking-cast boot.

His fault. Each of Ryland's muscles tensed in frustration. He should have known better than to be showboating during the friendly with Mexico. Now he was sidelined, unable to run or kick.

The media had accused him of being hungover or drunk when he hurt himself. They'd been wrong. Again. But dealing with the press was as much a part of his job as what happened for ninety minutes out on the pitch.

He'd appeared on camera, admitted the reason for his

injury—goofing off for the fans and the cameras—and apologized to both fans and teammates. But the truth had made him look more like a bad boy than ever given his red cards during matches the last couple of seasons, the trouble he'd gotten into off the field and the endless "reports" on his dating habits.

The dog whined louder.

From soccer superstar to dog sitter. Ryland half laughed.

Cupcake barked, as if tired of being put off any longer.

"Come here," Ryland said.

His parents' small dog pranced across the padded gym floor, acting more like a pedigreed champion show dog than a full-blooded mutt. Ryland had wanted to buy his mom and dad a purebred, but they adopted a dog from the local animal shelter, instead.

Cupcake stared up at him with sad, pitiful brown eyes. She had mangy gray fur, short legs and a long, bushy tail. Only his parents could love an animal this ugly and pathetic.

"Come on, girl." Ryland scooped her up into his arms. "I know you miss Mom and Dad. I do, too. But you need to stop crying. They deserve a vacation without having to worry about you or me."

He'd given his parents a cruise for their thirty-second wedding anniversary. Even though he'd bought them this mansion on the opposite side of town, far away from the two-bedroom apartment where he'd grown up, and deposited money into a checking account for them each month, both continued to work in the same low-paying jobs they'd had for as long as their marriage. They also drove the same old vehicles even though newer ones, Christmas presents from him, were parked in the four-car garage.

His parents' sole indulgence was Cupcake. They spoiled the dog rotten. They hadn't wanted to leave her in a kennel or in the care of a stranger while away so after his injury they asked Ryland if he would dog sit. His parents never asked him for anything so he'd jumped at the opportunity to do this.

Ryland hated being back in Wicksburg. There were too many

bad memories from when he was a kid. Even small towns had bullies and not-so-nice cliques.

He missed the fun and excitement of a big city, but he needed time to get away to repair the damage he'd done to his foot and his reputation. No one was happy with him at the moment, especially himself. Until getting hurt, he hadn't realized he'd been so restless, unfocused, careless.

Cupcake pawed at his hands. Her sign she wanted rubs.

"Mom and Dad will be home before you know it." Ryland petted the top of her head. "Okay?"

The dog licked him.

He placed her on the floor then stood. "I'm getting some water. Then it's shower time. If I don't shave, I'm going to start looking mangy like you."

Cupcake barked.

His cell phone, sitting on the countertop next to his water bottle, rang. He read the name on the screen. Blake Cochrane. His agent.

Ryland glanced at the clock. Ten o'clock here meant seven o'clock in Los Angeles. "An early morning for you."

"I'm here by six to beat the traffic," Blake said. "According to Twitter, you made a public appearance the other night. I thought we agreed you were going to lay low."

"I was hungry. The fire station was having their annual spaghetti feed so I thought I could eat and support a good cause. They asked if I'd sign autographs and pose for pictures. I couldn't say no."

"Any press?"

"The local weekly paper." With the phone in one hand and a water bottle in the other, Ryland walked to the living room with Cupcake tagging alongside him. He tried hard not to favor his right foot. He'd only been off crutches a few days. "But I told them no interview because I wanted the focus to be on the event. The photographer took a few pictures of the crowd so I might be in one."

"Let's hope whatever is published is positive," Blake said.

"I was talking with people I grew up with." Some of the

same people who'd treated him like garbage until he'd joined a soccer team. Most accepted him after he became a starter on the high-school varsity team as a freshman. He'd shown them all by becoming a professional athlete. "I was surrounded by a bunch of happy kids."

"That sounds safe enough," Blake admitted. "But be careful. Another endorsement deal fell through. They're nervous about your injury. The concerns over your image didn't help."

Ryland dragged his hand through his hair. "Let me guess. They want a clean-cut American, not a bad boy who thinks red cards are better than goals."

"You got it," Blake said. "I haven't heard anything official, but rumors are swirling that Mr. McElroy wants to loan you out to a Premier League team."

McElroy was the new owner of the Phoenix Fuego, who took more interest in players and team than any other head honcho in the MLS. He'd fired the coach/manager who'd wanted to run things his way and hired a new coach, Elliot Fritz, who didn't mind the owner being so hands-on. "Seriously?"

"I've heard it from more than one source."

Damn. As two teams were mentioned, Ryland plopped into his dad's easy chair. Cupcake jumped onto his lap.

"I took my eye off the ball," he said. "I made some mistakes. I apologized. I'm recovering and keeping my name out of the news. I don't see why we all can't move on."

"It's not that easy. You're one of the best soccer players in the world. Before your foot surgery, you were a first-team player who could have started for any team here or abroad. Not many American footballers can say that," Blake said. "But McElroy believes your bad-boy image isn't a draw in the stands or with the kids. Merchandising is important these days."

"Yeah, I know. Being injured and getting older isn't helping my cause." As if twenty-nine made Ryland an old man. He remembered what the team owner had said in an interview. "McElroy called me an overpaid liability. But if that's the case, why would an overseas team want to take me on?"

"The transfer period doesn't start until June. None have said they want the loan yet."

Ouch. Ryland knew he had only himself to blame for the mess he found himself in.

"The good news is the MLS doesn't want to lose a home-grown player as talented as you. McElroy's feathers got ruffled," Blake continued. "He's asserting his authority and reminding you that he controls your contract."

"You mean, my future."

"That's how billionaires are."

"I'll stick to being a millionaire, then."

Blake sighed.

"Look, I get why McElroy's upset. Coach Fritz, too. I haven't done a good job handling stuff," Ryland admitted. "I'll be the first to admit I've never been an angel. But I'm not the devil, either. There's no way I could do everything the press says I do. The media exaggerates everything."

"True, but people's concerns are real. This time at your parents' house is critical. Watch yourself."

"I'm going to fix this. I want to play in the MLS." Ryland had already done an eleven-year stint in the U.K. "My folks are doing fine, but they're not getting any younger. I don't want to be an ocean away from them. If McElroy doesn't want me, see if the Indianapolis Rage or another club does."

"McElroy isn't going to let a franchise player like you go to another MLS team," Blake said matter-of-factly. "If you want to play stateside, it'll be with Fuego."

Ryland petted Cupcake. "Then I'll have to keep laying low and polishing my image so it shines."

"Blind me, Ry."

"Will do." Everyone always wanted something from him. This was no different. But it sucked he had to prove himself all over again with Mr. McElroy and the Phoenix fans. "At least I can't get into trouble dog sitting. Wicksburg is the definition of boring."

"Women—"

"Not here," Ryland interrupted. "I know what's expected of

me. I also know it's hard on my mom to read the gossip about me on the internet. She doesn't need to hear it firsthand from women in town."

"You should bring your mom back with you to Phoenix."

"Dude. Keeping it quiet and on the down low is fine while I'm here, but let's not go crazy," Ryland said. "In spite of the reports of me hooking up with every starlet in Hollywood, I've been more than discreet and discriminate with whom I see. But beautiful women coming on to me are one of the perks of the sport."

Blake sighed. "I remember when you were this scrappy, young kid who cared about nothing but soccer. It used to be all about the game for you."

"It's still about the game." Ryland was the small-town kid from the Midwest who hit the big-time overseas, playing with the best in the world. Football, as they called it everywhere but in the U.S., meant everything to him. Without it... "Soccer is my life. That's why I'm trying to get back on track."

A beat passed and another. "Just remember, actions speak louder than words."

After a quick goodbye, Blake disconnected from the call.

Ryland stared at his phone. He'd signed with Blake when he was eighteen. The older Ryland got, the smarter his agent's advice sounded.

Actions speak louder than words.

Lately his actions hadn't been any more effective than his words. He looked at Cupcake. "I've put myself in the doghouse. Now I've got to get myself out of it."

The doorbell rang.

Cupcake jumped off his lap and ran to the front door barking ferociously, as if she weighed ninety pounds, not nineteen.

Who could that be? He wasn't expecting anyone.

The dog kept barking. He remained seated.

Let Cupcake deal with whomever was at the door. If he ignored them, maybe they would go away. The last thing Ryland wanted right now was company.

CHAPTER TWO

Lucy's hand hovered over the mansion's doorbell. She fought the urge to press the button a third time. She didn't want to annoy Mr. and Mrs. James. Yes, she wanted to get this fool's errand over with, but appearing overeager or worse, rude, wouldn't help her find a coach for Connor's team.

"Come on," she muttered. "Open the door."

The constant high-pitch yapping of a dog suggested the doorbell worked. But that didn't explain why no one had answered yet. Maybe the house was so big it took them a long time to reach the front door. Lucy gripped the container of cookies with both hands.

The dog continued barking.

Maybe no one was home. She rose up on her tiptoes and peeked through the four-inch strip of small leaded-glass squares on the ornate wood door.

Lights shone inside.

Someone had to be home. Leaving the lights on when away wasted electricity. Her dad used to tell her that. Aaron said the same thing to Connor. But she supposed if a person could afford to live in an Architectural Digest–worthy home with its Georgian-inspired columns, circular drive and manicured lawn that looked like a green carpet, they probably didn't worry about paying the electricity bill.

Lucy didn't see anyone coming toward the door. She couldn't see the dog, either. She lowered her heels to the welcome mat.

Darn it. She didn't want to come back later and try again. A chill shivered down her spine. She needed to calm down.

She imagined Connor with a smile on his face and soccer cleats on his feet. Her anxiety level dropped.

If no one answered, she would return. She would keep coming back until she spoke with Ryland James.

The dog's barking became more agitated.

A sign? Probably not, but she might as well ring the bell once more before calling it quits.

She pressed the doorbell. A symphony of chimes erupted into a Mozart tune. At least the song sounded like Mozart the third time hearing it.

The door opened slightly. A little gray dog darted out and sniffed her shoes. The pup placed its stubby front paws against her jean-covered calves.

"Off, Cupcake." The dog ran to the grass in the front yard. A man in navy athletic shorts with a black walking-cast on his right leg stood in the doorway. "She's harmless."

The dog might be, but not him.

Ryland James.

Hot. Sexy. Oh, my.

He looked like a total bad boy with his short, brown hair damp and mussed, as if he hadn't taken time to comb it after he crawled out of bed. Shaving didn't seem to be part of his morning routine, either. He used to be so clean-cut and all-American, but the dark stubble covering his chin and cheeks gave him an edge. His bare muscular chest glistened as if he'd just finished a workout. He had a tattoo on his right biceps and another on the backside of his left wrist. His tight, underwear model–worthy abs drew her gaze lower. Her mouth went dry.

Lucy forced her gaze up and stared into the hazel eyes that had once fueled her teenage daydreams. His dark lashes seemed even thicker. How was that possible?

The years had been good, very good to him. The guy was more gorgeous than ever with his classically handsome features, ones that had become more defined, almost refined, with age. His nose, however, looked as if it had been broken at least once. Rather than detract from his looks, his nose gave him character, made him appear more...rugged. Manly. Dangerous.

Lucy's heart thudded against her ribs. "It's you."

"I'm me." His lips curved into a charming smile, sending her already-racing pulse into a mad sprint. "You're not what I expected to find on my doorstep, but my day's looking a whole lot better now."

Her turn. But Lucy found herself tongue-tied. The same way she'd been whenever he was over at her house years ago. Her gaze strayed once again to his amazing abs. Wowza.

"You okay?" he asked.

Remember Connor. She raised her chin. "I was expecting—"

"One of my parents."

She nodded.

"I was hoping you were here to see me," he said.

"I am." The words rushed from her lips like water from Connor's Super Soaker gun. She couldn't let nerves get the best of her now that she'd accomplished the first part of her mission and was standing face-to-face with Ryland. "But I thought one of them would answer the door since you're injured."

"They would have if they'd been home." His rich, deep voice, as smooth and warm as a mug of hot cocoa, flowed over her. "I'm Ryland James."

"I know."

"That puts me at a disadvantage because I don't know who you are."

"I meant, I know you. But it was a long time ago," she clarified.

His gaze raked over her. "I would remember meeting you."

Lucy was used to guys hitting on her. She hadn't expected that from Ryland, but she liked it. Other men's attention annoyed her. His flirting made her feel attractive and desired.

"Let me take a closer look to see if I can jog my memory," he said.

The approval in his eyes gave her goose bumps. The good kind, ones she hadn't felt in a while. She hadn't wanted to jump back into the dating scene after her divorce two years ago.

"I *have* seen that pretty smile of yours before," he continued. "Those sparkling blue eyes, too."

Oh, boy. Her knees felt wobbly. Tingles filled her stomach. *Stop.* She wasn't back in middle school.

Lucy straightened. The guy hadn't a clue who she was. Ryland James was a professional athlete. Knowing what to say to women was probably part of their training camp.

"I'm Lucy." For some odd reason, she sounded husky. She cleared her throat. "Lucy Martin."

"Lucy." Lines creased Ryland's forehead. "Aaron Martin's little sister?"

She nodded.

"Same smile and blue eyes, but everything else has changed." Ryland's gaze ran the length of her again. "Just look at you now."

She braced herself, waiting to hear how sick she'd been and how ugly she'd looked before her liver transplant.

He grinned. "Little Lucy is all grown up now."

Little Lucy? She stiffened. His words confused her. She hadn't been little. Okay, maybe when they first met back in elementary school. But she'd been huge, a bloated whale, and yellow due to jaundice the last time he'd seen her. "It's been what? Thirteen years since we last saw each other."

"Thirteen years too long," he said.

What was going on? Old crushes were supposed to get fat and lose their hair, not get even hotter and appear interested in you. He sounded interested. Unless her imagination was getting the best of her.

No, she knew better when it came to men. "It looks as if life is treating you well. Except for your leg—"

"Foot. Nothing serious."

"You had surgery."

"A minor inconvenience, that's all. Nothing like what you suffered through," he said. "The liver transplant seems to have done what Aaron hoped it would do. All he ever wanted was for you to be healthy."

"I am." She wondered why Aaron would have talked about

her illness to Ryland. All they'd cared about were soccer and girls. Well, every other girl in Wicksburg except her. "I take medicine each day and have a monthly blood test, but otherwise I'm the same as everybody else."

"No, you're not." Ryland's gaze softened. "There's nothing ordinary about you. Never has been. It sucked that you were sick, but you were always so brave."

Heat stole up her neck toward her cheeks. Butterflies flapped in her tummy. Her heart...

Whoa-whoa-whoa. Don't get carried away by a few nice words from a good-looking guy, even if that guy happened to be the former man of her dreams. She'd been a naive kid back then. She'd learned the hard way that people said things they didn't mean. They lied, even after saying how much they loved you. Lucy squared her shoulders.

Time to get this over with. She handed Ryland the cookies. "These are for you."

He removed the container's lid. His brows furrowed. "Cookies?"

Ryland sounded surprised. She bit the inside of her mouth, hoping he liked them. "Chocolate chip."

"My favorite. Thanks."

He seemed pleased. Good. "Aaron's son, Connor, helped me make them. He's nine and loves soccer. That's why I'm here. To ask a favor."

Ryland looked at the cookies, then at her. "I appreciate your honesty. Not many people are so up-front when they want something. Let's talk inside."

She hesitated, unsure of the wisdom of going into the house. Once upon a time she'd believed in happily ever after and one true love. But life had taught her those things belonged only in fairy tales. Love and romance were overrated. But Ryland was making her feel things she tried hard not to think about too much—attraction, desire, hope.

But the other part of her, the part that tended to be impulsive and had gotten her into trouble more than once, was curious. She wanted to know if his parents' house was as nice on the inside as the exterior and front yard. Heaven knew she would never live in an exclusive neighborhood like this one. This might be her only chance to find out.

Ryland leaned against the doorway. The casual pose took weight off his right foot. He might need to sit down.

"Sure." She didn't want him hurting. "That would be nice."

He whistled for the dog.

Cupcake ran inside.

Lucy entered the house. The air was cooler than outside and smelled lemony. Wood floors gleamed. A giant chandelier hung from the twenty-foot ceiling in the foyer. She clamped her lips together so her mouth wouldn't gape. Original water-color paintings in gilded frames decorated the textured walls. Tasteful and expensive.

She stepped through a wide-arched doorway into the living room. Talk about beautiful. The yellow and green décor was light, bright and inviting. The colors, fabrics and accessories coordinated perfectly. What she liked most was how comfortable the room looked, not at all like some of those unlivable magazine layouts or model homes.

Family pictures sat on the wooden-fireplace mantle. A framed poster-size portrait of Ryland, wearing a U.S. National team uniform, hung on the wall. An open paperback novel rested cover-side up on an end table. "Your parents' house is lovely."

"Thanks."

He sounded proud, making her wonder about his part in his parents' house. She'd guess a big part, given his solid relationship with his mom and dad when he'd been a teen.

"My mom thought the house was too big, but I convinced her she deserved it after so many years of apartment living." Ryland motioned to a sofa. "Have a seat."

Lucy sat, sinking into the overstuffed cushions. More comfortable than the futon she'd sold before leaving Chicago. She'd gotten rid of her few pieces of furniture so she wouldn't have to pay for storage while living at Aaron and Dana's house.

Cupcake hopped up next to her.

"Is she allowed on the couch?" Lucy asked.

"The dog is allowed everywhere except the dining-room table and kitchen counters. She belongs to my parents. They've spoiled her rotten." Ryland sounded more amused than angry. He sat on a wingback chair to her right. "Mind if I have a cookie?"

"Please do."

He offered her the container. "Would you like one?"

The chocolate chips smelled good, but she would be eating cookies with Connor later. Better not overdo the sweets. The trips to the ice-cream parlor and Rocket Burger with her nephew were already adding up. "No, thanks."

Ryland took one. "I can't remember the last time someone baked anything for me."

"What about your mom?"

"I don't spend as much time with my parents as I'd like due to soccer. Right now I'm dog sitting while they're away." Cupcake circled around as if chasing her own tail, then plopped against the cushion and placed her head on Lucy's thigh. "She likes you."

Lucy ran her fingers through the soft gray fur. She'd never had a dog. "She's sweet."

"When she wants to be." Ryland bit into the cookie. He took his time eating it. "Delicious."

The cookies were a hit. Lucy hoped they worked as a bribe. She mustered her courage. Not that she could back out now even if she wanted to. "So my nephew..."

"Does he want an autograph?" Ryland placed the cookie container on the coffee table. "Maybe a team jersey or ball?"

"Connor would love it if you signed his ball, but what he really wants is a coach for his spring under-9 rec. team." She didn't want to waste any more of Ryland's time. Or hers. "He wanted me to ask if you could coach his team, the Defeeters."

Ryland flinched. "Me? Coach?"

"I know that's a big request and likely impossible for you to do right now."

He looked at his injured foot. "Yeah, this isn't a good time. I hope to be back with my team in another month or so."

"I'm sure you will be. Aaron says you're one of the best players in the world."

"Thanks. It's just… I'm supposed to be laying low while I'm here. Staying out of the press. The media could turn my coaching your nephew's team into a circus." Ryland stared at the dog. "I'm really sorry I can't help you out."

"No worries. I told Connor you probably couldn't coach." Lucy knew Ryland would never say yes. He'd left his small-town roots behind and become famous, traveling all over the U.S. and the world. The exotic lifestyle was as foreign to her as the game of soccer itself. But maybe she could get him to agree to something else that wouldn't take so much of his time. "But if you happen to have an hour to spare sometime, Connor and his teammates would be thrilled if you could give them a pep talk."

Silence stretched between them. She'd put him on the spot with that request, too. But she'd had no choice if she wanted to help her nephew.

"I can do that," Ryland said finally.

Lucy released the breath she hadn't realized she was holding. "Thanks."

"I'm happy to talk to them, sign balls, pose for pictures, whatever the boys want."

She hoped the visit would appease Connor. "That will be great. Thanks."

Ryland's eyes darkened, more brown than hazel now. "Who will you get to coach?"

"I don't know," she admitted. "Practices don't start until next week so I still have a little time left to find someone. I can always coach, if need be."

Surprise flashed across his face. "You play soccer?"

Lucy hadn't been allowed to do anything physical when she was younger. Even though she no longer had any physical limitations, she preferred art to athletics. "No, but I've been reading up on the game and watching video clips on the internet, just in case."

His lips narrowed. "Aaron was great with those kids when we put on that camp back in high school. Why doesn't he coach the team?"

"Aaron's coached the Defeeters for years, but he's overseas right now with the army. Both he and his wife were deployed with their Reserve unit last month. I'm taking care of Connor until they return next year."

"Aaron talked about using the military to pay for college," Ryland said thoughtfully. "But I lost track of him, of everyone, when I left Wicksburg."

"He joined the army right after high school." Lucy's medical expenses had drained their college funds, her parents' saving account and the equity in their house. Sometimes it felt as if she was still paying for the transplant years later. Aaron, too. "That's where he met his wife, Dana. After they completed their Active Duty, they joined the Reserves."

"A year away from home. Away from their son." Ryland dragged his hand through his hair. "That has to be rough."

Lucy's chest tightened. "You do what you have to do."

"Still…"

"You left home to go to Florida and then England."

"To play soccer. Not protect my country," Ryland said. "I had the time of my life. I doubt Aaron and his wife can say the same thing right now."

Lucy remembered the tears glistening in Connor's eyes as he told her his mom sounded like she was crying on the phone. "You're right about that."

"I respect what Aaron and his wife, what all of the military, are doing. The sacrifices they make. True heroes. Every one of them."

Ryland sounded earnest. She wanted to believe he was sincere. Maybe he was still a small-town guy at heart. "They are."

Cupcake rolled over on her back. She waved her front paws in the air.

Lucy took the not-so-subtle hint and rubbed the dog's stomach.

"So you've stuck around Wicksburg," Ryland said.

"I left for a while. College. I also lived in Chicago." Aaron had accused her of running away when her marriage failed. Maybe he'd been right. But she'd had to do something when her life crumbled around her. "I moved back last month."

"To care for your nephew."

She nodded. "Saying no never entered into my mind. Not after everything Aaron has done for me."

"He was so protective of you."

"He still is."

"That doesn't surprise me." Ryland rubbed his thigh above the brace he wore. He rested his foot on an ottoman. "Did you leave your boyfriend behind in Chi-town or did he come with you?"

She drew back, surprised by the question. "I, uh, don't have a boyfriend."

He grinned wryly. "So you need a soccer coach and a boyfriend. I hope your brother told you the right qualities to look for in each."

Aaron always gave her advice, but she hadn't always listened to him. Lucy should have done so before eloping. She couldn't change the past. But she wouldn't make that same mistakes again.

"A soccer coach is all I need." Lucy figured Ryland had to be teasing her, but this wasn't a joking matter. She needed a boyfriend as much as she needed another ex-husband. She shifted positions. "I have my hands full with Connor. He's my priority. A kid should be happy and carefree, not frowning and down all the time."

"Maybe we should get him together with Cupcake," Ryland said. "She goes from being happy to sad. I'm a poor substitute for my parents."

Lucy's insecurities rushed to the surface. She never thought she would have something in common with him. "That's how I feel with Connor. Nothing I do seems to be…enough."

Ryland leaned forward. His large hand engulfed hers. His touch was light. His skin was warm. "Hey. You're here to see me about his team. That says a lot. Aaron and his family, especially Connor, are lucky to have you."

Ryland's words wrapped around Lucy like a big hug. But his touch disturbed her more than it comforted. Heat emanated from the point of contact and spread up her arm. She tried not to think about it. "I'm the lucky one."

"Maybe some of that luck will rub off on me."

"Your injury?" she asked.

"Yeah, and a few other things."

His hand still rested upon hers. Lucy hadn't been touched by a man in over two years. It felt...good.

Better not get used to it. Reluctantly, she pulled her hand from beneath his and reached for her purse.

"If you need some luck, I've got just the thing for you." Lucy removed a penny from her change pocket and gave it to Ryland. "My grammy told me this is all a person needs to get lucky."

Wicked laughter lit his eyes. "Here I thought it took a killer opening line, oodles of charm and an expensive bottle of champagne."

Oh, no. Lucy realized what she'd said. Her cheeks burned. "I meant to change their luck."

He winked. "I know, but you gave me the opening. I had to take the shot."

At least he hadn't scored. Not yet, anyway. Lucy swallowed.

"Aaron would have done the same." She needed to be careful, though. Ryland was charming, but he wasn't her big brother. Being near him short-circuited her brain. She couldn't think straight. That was bad. The last time she allowed herself to be charmed by a man she'd ended up with a wedding ring on her finger.

"You said your nephew loves soccer," Ryland said.

She nodded, thankful for the change in subject. "Yes. Connor and Aaron are crazy about the sport. They wear matching jerseys. It's cute, though Dana says it's annoying when they get up at some crazy hour to watch a game in Europe. But I don't think she minds that much."

Lucy cringed at her rambling. Ryland didn't care about Aaron's family's infatuation with soccer. She needed to shut up. Now.

"That's great they're so into the game." A thoughtful expression crossed Ryland's face. "I haven't been back in town for a while, but I bet some of the same people are still involved in soccer. I'll ask around to see if there's someone who can coach your nephew's team."

Her mouth parted in surprise. She liked being self-reliant and hated asking for help, but in this case Ryland had offered. She'd be stupid to say no when this meant so much to Connor. "I'd appreciate that. If it's not too much trouble."

"No trouble. I'm happy to do it. Anything for…"

You, she thought.

"…Aaron."

Of course, this was for her brother. Ryland's childhood and high-school friend and teammate. She ignored the twinge of disappointment. "Thanks."

Ryland held the penny between the pads of his thumb and index finger. "You've made me cookies, given me a lucky penny. What do I get if I find a coach?"

Lucy wondered if he was serious or teasing her. His smile suggested the latter. "My undying gratitude?"

"That's a good start."

"More cookies?"

"Always appreciated, especially if they're chocolate chip," he said. "What else?"

His lighthearted and flirty tone sounded warning bells in her head. Ryland *was* teasing her, but Lucy no longer wanted to play along. His charm, pretty much everything about him, unsettled her. "I'm not sure what else you might want."

He gave her the once-over, only this time his gaze lingered a second too long on her lips. "I can think of a couple things."

So could Lucy. The man was smokin' hot. His lips looked as if they could melt her insides with one kiss. Sex appeal oozed from him.

A good thing she'd sworn off men because she could tell the

soccer pitch wasn't the only place where Ryland James played. Best not to even start that game. She'd only lose. Again.

Not. Going. To. Happen.

Time to steer this conversation back to where it needed to be so she could get out of here.

"How about you make a list?" Lucy kept a smile on her face and her tone light and friendly. After all, he was going to try to find Connor's team a coach. But if Ryland thought she was going to swoon at his feet in adoration and awe, he had another think coming. "If you find the team a coach, we'll go from there."

Ryland's smile crinkled the corner of his eyes, taking her breath away. "I always thought you were a cool kid, Lucy Martin, but I really like who you are now."

Okay, she was attracted to him. Any breathing female with a pulse would be. The guy was appealing with a capital *A*.

But Lucy wasn't stupid. She knew the type. His type.

Ryland James spelled T-R-O-U-B-L-E.

Once he visited the Defeeters, she never wanted to see him again. And she wouldn't.

It was so good to see Lucy Martin again.

Ryland sat in the living room waiting for her to return with Cupcake, who needed to go outside. Lucy had offered to take the dog to the backyard so he wouldn't have to get up. He'd agreed if only to keep her here a little while longer.

He couldn't get over the difference in her.

She'd been a shy, sweet girl with freckles, long braids and yellowish whites surrounding her huge blue eyes. Now she was a confident, sweet woman with a glowing complexion, strawberry-blond hair worn in a short and sassy style, and mesmerizing sky-blue eyes.

Ryland had been wrong about not wanting company this morning. Sure she'd shown up because she wanted something. But she'd brought him cookies—a bribe, no doubt—and been straightforward asking him for a favor.

He appreciated and respected that.

Some women were devious and played up to him to get what they wanted. Lucy hadn't even wanted something for herself, but for her nephew. That was…refreshing.

Cupcake ran into the living room and hopped onto the couch.

Lucy took her same spot next to the dog. "Sorry that took so long, the dog wanted to run around before she got down to business."

"Thanks for taking her out." Lucy had brightened Ryland's mood, making him smile and laugh. He wanted her to stick around. "You must be thirsty. I'll get you something to drink. Coffee? Water? A soda?"

Lucy shifted on the couch. "No, thanks."

Years ago, Aaron had told Ryland that his sister had a crush on him so to be nice to her. He had been. Now he was curious to know if any of her crush remained. "It's no trouble."

But he could get in trouble wondering if she were still interested in him. He was supposed to be avoiding women.

Not that he was pursuing her. Though he was…curious.

She grabbed her purse. "Thanks, but I should be going."

Lucy was different than other women he knew. Most would kill for that kind of invitation from him, but she didn't seem impressed or want to hang out with him. She'd eagerly taken Cupcake outside while he stayed inside. Almost as if she'd wanted some distance from him.

Interesting. His charm and fame usually melted whatever feminine resistance he faced. Not with Lucy. He kind of liked the idea of a challenge. Not that it could go anywhere, he reminded himself. "I'd like to hear more about Aaron."

"Perhaps another time."

"You have somewhere to be?"

Her fingers curled around the leather strap. "I have work to do before Connor gets home from school."

Ryland would have liked it if she stayed longer, but he would see her again. No doubt about that. He rose. "I'll see you out."

She stood. Her purse swung like a pendulum. "That's not necessary. Stay off your foot. I know where the door is."

"My foot can handle it."

Lucy's gaze met his. "I can see myself out."

He found the unwavering strength in her eyes a big turn-on. "I know, but I want to show you out."

After what felt like forever, she looked away with a shrug. "It's your foot."

He bit back a smile. She would be a challenge all right. A fun one. "Yes, it is."

Ryland accompanied Lucy to her car, a practical looking white, four-door subcompact. "Thanks for coming by and bringing me cookies. I'll give you a call about a coach and talking to the team."

She removed something from an outside pocket of her purse and handed it to him. "My cell-phone number is on my business card. Aaron has a landline, but this is the best way to reach me."

He stared at the purple card with white and light blue lettering and a swirly border. That looked more like Lucy. "Freelance graphic designer. So you're still into art."

"You remember that?"

She sounded incredulous, but the way her eyes danced told him she was also pleased.

"You'd be surprised what I remember."

Her lips parted once again.

He'd piqued her interest. Good, because she'd done the same to him. "But don't worry, it's all good."

A charming blush crept into Lucy's cheeks.

"We'll talk later." Ryland didn't want to make her uncomfortable, but flirting with her came so easily. "You have work to do now."

"Yes, I do." She dug around the inside of her purse. As she pulled out her keys, metal clanged against metal. "Thanks. I'm… I look forward to hearing from you."

"It won't be long." And it wouldn't. Ryland couldn't wait to talk to her again. "I promise."

CHAPTER THREE

THAT afternoon, the front door burst open with so much force Lucy thought a tornado had touched down in Wicksburg. She stood her ground in the living room, knowing this burst of energy wasn't due to Mother Nature—the warning siren hadn't gone off—but was man, er, boy-made.

Manny usually couldn't wait for Connor to get home and make another escape attempt, but the cat hightailed it into the kitchen. A ball of dark fur slid across the linoleum before disappearing from sight.

Connor flew into the house, strands of his strawberry-blond hair going every which way. He was lanky, the way his dad had been at that age, all limbs with not an ounce of fat on him. The set of his jaw and the steely determination in his eyes made him seem more superhero than a four-and-a-half-foot third grader. All he needed was a cape to wear over his jersey and jeans.

"Hey." Lucy knew he wanted to know about her visit to Ryland, but the sexy soccer player had been on her mind since she'd left him. Much to her dismay. She didn't want to start her time with Connor focused on the guy, too. "Did you have a good day at school? You had a spelling quiz, right?"

He slammed the front door closed. The entire house shook. His backpack hung precariously off one thin shoulder, but he didn't seem to care. "Did you talk to Ryland James?"

Connor had the same one-track mind as her brother. When Aaron had something he wanted to do, like joining the military, he defined tunnel vision.

Lucy might as well get this over with. "I went to Mr. and Mrs. James's house this morning. Ryland liked the cookies we baked."

The backpack thudded against the entryway's tile floor. Anticipation filled Connor's blue eyes. "Is he going to coach the Defeeters?"

This was the part she hadn't been looking forward to since leaving the Jameses' house. "No, but Ryland offered to see if he can find the team a coach. He's also going to come out and talk to the team."

Different emotions crossed Connor's face. Sadness, anger, surprise. A thoughtful expression settled on his features. "I guess he must be really busy."

"Ryland's trying to heal and stay in shape." Her temperature rose remembering how he looked in only a pair of shorts and gleam of sweat. "He doesn't plan on being in town long. Maybe a month or so. He wants to rejoin his team as soon as he can."

Manny peered around the doorway to the kitchen, saw Connor and ran to him.

Connor picked up the cat. "I guess I would want to do that, too."

Poor kid. He was trying to put on a brave face. She wished things could be different for him. "There's still time to find the Defeeters a coach."

He stared over the cat's head. "That's what you said last week. And the week before that."

"True, but now I have help looking for a coach." Lucy hoped Ryland had been serious about his offer and came through for... the boys. "A good thing, otherwise, you'll be stuck with me."

Connor nodded.

She ruffled his hair. "Gee, thanks."

"You're the one who said it." He flashed her a lopsided grin. "But no matter what happens, having you for a coach is better than not playing at all."

Lucy hoped he was right. "I'll do my best if it comes down to that."

"It won't." Connor sounded so confident.

"How do you know?"

"If Ryland James said he'd find us a coach, he will."

She'd been disappointed too many times to put that much faith into someone. Ryland had seemed sincere and enthusiastic. But so had others. Best not to raise Connor's hopes too high on the chance his favorite player didn't come through after all. "Ryland said he'd *try*. He's going to call me."

"Have you checked your voice mail yet?" Connor asked.

His eagerness made her smile. She'd been wondering when the call might come herself. They both needed to be realistic. "I just saw Ryland a couple hours ago."

"Hours? He could have found us five coaches by now."

She doubted that.

"All Ryland James has to do is snap his fingers and people will come running," Connor continued.

Lucy could imagine women running to the gorgeous Ryland. She wasn't so sure the same could be said about coaches. Not unless they were female.

"Check your cell phone," Connor encouraged.

The kid was relentless…like his dad. "Give Ryland time to snap his fingers. I mean, make calls. I know this is important to you, but a little patience here would be good."

"You could call him."

No, she couldn't. Wouldn't. "He said he'd call. Rushing him wouldn't be nice."

She also didn't want to give Ryland the wrong impression so he might think she was interested in him. A guy like him meant one thing—heartbreak. She'd had enough of that to last a lifetime.

"Let's give him at least a day, maybe two, to call us, okay?" she suggested.

"Okay," Connor agreed reluctantly.

She bit back a laugh. "How about some cookies and milk while you tell me about school?"

Maybe that would get Ryland James out of Connor's thoughts. And hers, too.

"Sure." As he walked toward the kitchen, he looked back at her. "So does Ryland James have a soccer field in his backyard?"

Lucy swallowed a sigh. And then maybe not.

After dinner, Ryland retreated with Cupcake into the media room aka his dad's man cave. He had all he needed—laptop, cell phone, chocolate-chip cookies, Lucy's business card and a seventy-inch LED television with ESPN playing. As soon as Ryland found Lucy a coach for her nephew's team, he would call her with the good news.

Forget the delicious cookies she'd made. The only dessert he wanted was to hear her sweet voice on the opposite end of the phone.

Ryland laughed. He must need some feminine attention if he felt this way.

But seeing Lucy again had made him feel good. She also had him thinking about the past. Many of his childhood memories living in Wicksburg were like bad dreams, ones he'd pushed to the far recesses of his mind and wanted to keep there. But a few others, like the ones he remembered now, brought a welcome smile to his face.

Cupcake lay on an Indianapolis Colts dog bed.

Even though Ryland played soccer, his dad preferred football, the American kind. But his dad had never once tried to change Ryland's mind about what sport to play. Instead, his father had done all he could so Ryland could succeed in the sport. He would be nowhere without his dad and his mom.

And youth soccer.

He'd learned the basic skills and the rules of the game playing in the same rec. league Aaron's son played in. When Ryland moved to a competitive club, playing up a year from his own age group, his dad's boss, Mr. Buckley, who owned a local farm, bought Ryland new cleats twice a year. Not cheap ones, but the good kind. Mr. Martin, Aaron and Lucy's dad, would drive Ryland to away games and tournaments when his parents had to work.

Lucy taking care of Aaron's son didn't surprise Ryland. The Martins had always been a loyal bunch.

In elementary school, other kids used to taunt him. Aaron stood up for Ryland even before they were teammates. Once they started playing on the same team, they became good friends. But Ryland had wanted to put Wicksburg behind him when he left.

And he had.

He'd focused all his effort and energy into being the best soccer player he could be.

Now that he was back in town, finding a soccer coach was the least he could do for his old friend Aaron. Ryland pressed the mute button on the television's remote then picked up his cell phone. This wouldn't take long.

Two hours later, he disconnected from yet another call. He couldn't believe it. No matter whom he'd spoken with, the answer was still the same—no. Only the reason for not being able to coach changed.

"Wish I could help you out, Ryland, but I'm already coaching two other teams."

"Gee, if I'd known sooner…"

"Try the high school. Maybe one of the students could do it as a class project or something."

Ryland placed his cell phone on the table. Even the suggestion to contact the high school had led to a dead end. No wonder Lucy had asked him to coach Connor's team.

Ryland looked at Cupcake. "What am I going to do?"

The dog kept her eyes closed.

"Go ahead. Pretend you don't hear me. That's what everyone else has done tonight."

Okay, not quite. His calling had resulted in four invitations to dinner and five requests to speak to soccer teams. Amazing how things and his status in town had changed. All his hard work had paid off. Though he was having to start over with Mr. McElroy and the Fuego.

"I need to find Lucy a coach."

Cupcake stretched.

Something flashed on the television screen. Highlights from a soccer match.

Yearning welled inside him. He missed the action on the field, the adrenaline pushing through him to run faster and the thrill of taking the ball toward the goal and scoring. Thinking about playing soccer was making him nostalgic for days when kids, a ball and some grass defined the game in its simplest and purest form.

Lucy's business card caught his eye.

Attraction flared to life. He wanted to talk to her. Now.

Ryland picked up his cell phone. He punched in the first three digits of her number then placed the phone back on the table.

Calling her tonight would be stupid. Saying he wanted to hear her voice might be true, but he didn't want to push too hard and scare her off. Other women might love a surprise phone call, but Lucy might not. She wasn't like the women he dated.

That, he realized, surprisingly appealed to him. Sitting in his parents' living room eating cookies and talking with a small-town girl had energized him in a way no visit to a top restaurant or trendy club with a date ever had.

Ryland stared at the cell phone. He wanted to talk to her, but if he called her he would have to admit his inability to find her a coach. That wouldn't go over well.

With him, he realized with a start. Lucy wouldn't be upset. She'd thank him for his efforts then take on the coaching role herself.

I can always coach, if need be.

You play soccer?

No, but I've been reading up on the game and watching coaching clips on the internet just in case.

He imagined her placing a whistle around her graceful neck and leading a team of boys at practice. Coaching would be nothing compared to what Lucy went through when she was sick. She would figure out the basics of what needed to be done and give the boys her all.

But she shouldn't *have* to do that. She was doing enough taking care of her nephew. The same as Aaron and his wife.

His gaze focused on Lucy's name on her business card. The script might be artistic and a touch whimsical, but it showed strength and ingenuity, too.

Ryland straightened. He couldn't let people saying no stop him. He was tougher than that. "I might have screwed up my career, but I'm not going to mess up this."

The dog stared at him.

"I'll find Lucy and those kids a coach."

No matter what he had to do.

Two days later, Lucy stood in the front yard kicking a soccer ball to Connor. The afternoon sun shone high in the sky, but the weather might as well be cloudy and gray due to the frown on her nephew's face. Practices began next week and the Defeeters still didn't have a coach. Ryland hadn't called back, either.

She tapped the ball with her left foot. It rolled too far to the left, out of Connor's reach and into the hedge separating the yard from the neighbor's. Lucy grimaced. "Sorry."

Connor didn't say a word but chased the ball. She knew what he was thinking because his expression matched her thoughts. The team needed someone who knew soccer better than she did, someone who could teach the kids the right skills and knew rules without having to resort to a book each time.

Her efforts to find a coach had failed. That left one person who could come to her—and the team's—rescue.

It won't be long. I promise.

Ryland's words returned to her in a rush. Pathetic, how quick she'd been to believe them. As if she hadn't learned anything based on her past experiences.

Okay, it had been only a couple of days. "Long" could mean a few days, a week, even a month. But "promise" was a seven-letter word that held zero weight with most of the people in this world.

Was Ryland one of them?

Time would tell, but for Connor's sake she hoped not. He kicked the ball back to her.

She stopped the ball with her right foot the way she'd seen someone do on a video then used the inside of her foot to kick the ball back. She had better control this time. "Your teacher liked your book report."

"I guess."

"You got an A."

Connor kicked the ball her way without stopping it first. "Are you sure he hasn't called?"

He equaled Ryland. Connor had been asking that question nonstop, including a call during lunchtime using a classmate's cell phone.

Lucy patted her jeans pocket. "My phone's right here."

"You checked your messages?"

"I did." And rechecked them. No messages from Ryland. From anyone for that matter. She hadn't made any close friends in Chicago. The ones who lived in Wicksburg had remained friends with her ex-husband after Lucy moved away. That made things uncomfortable now that she was back. The pity in their eyes reminded her of when she'd been sick. She wanted no part of that ever again. "But it's only been a couple of days."

"It feels like forever."

"I know." Each time her cell phone rang, thinking it might be Ryland filled her stomach with tingles of anticipation. She hated that. She didn't want to feel that way about any guy calling her, even if the reason was finding a coach for her nephew's soccer team. "But good things come to those who wait."

Connor rolled the ball back and forth along the bottom of his foot. "That's what Mom and Dad say. I'm trying to be patient, but it's hard."

"I know it's hard to wait, but we have to give Ryland time." Connor nodded.

Please come through, Ryland. Lucy didn't want Connor's favorite player letting him down at the worst possible time. She didn't want her nephew to have to face the kind of betrayal and disappointment she'd suffered due to others. Not when he was only nine, separated from his parents by oceans and continents.

He kicked the ball to her. "Maybe Ryland forgot."

Lucy didn't want to go there. The ball rolled past her toward the sidewalk. She chased after it. "Give him the benefit of the doubt."

Connor didn't say anything.

She needed him to stop focusing so much on Ryland. "Your dad wants to see videotapes of your games. He can't wait to see how the team does this spring."

She kicked the ball back. Connor touched the ball twice with his foot before kicking it to her.

"Next time only one touch," she said.

Surprise filled his blue eyes. "That's what my dad says."

"It might come as a shock, but your aunt knows a few things about the game of soccer." She'd found a book on coaching on the living-room bookcase and attended a coaching clinic put on by the league last night while Connor had dinner over at a friend's house. "How about we kick the ball a few times more, then go to the pizza parlor for dinner? You can play those video games you like so much."

"Okay."

Talk about an unenthused reaction.

An old beat-up, blue pickup truck pulled to the curb in front of the house. The engine idled loudly, as if in need of a tune-up. The engine sputtered off. The truck lurched forward a foot, maybe two.

The driver's door opened. Ryland.

Her heart thumped.

It won't be long. I promise.

Tingles filled her stomach. He hadn't let her down. He was still the same nice guy he'd been in high school.

Ryland rounded the front of the truck. He wore a white polo shirt with the Fuego logo on the left side, a pair of khaki shorts and the boot on his right foot. He wore a tennis shoe on his left. His hair was nicely styled. He'd shaved, removing the sexy stubble.

Even with his clean-cut look, she knew not to let her guard down. The guy was still dangerous. The only reason she was happy to see him was Connor.

A little voice inside her head laughed at that. She ignored it.

"It's him." Awe filled Connor's voice. "Ryland James."

"Yes, it's him," she said.

Ryland crossed the sidewalk and stood near them on the lawn. "Hello."

Lucy fought the urge to step back and put some distance between them. "Hi."

He acknowledged her with a nod, but turned his attention to the kid with the stars in his eyes. "You must be Connor."

Her nephew nodded.

Lucy's heart melted. Ryland knew how important this moment must be for her nephew.

Connor wiped his right hand against his shorts then extended his arm. "It's nice to meet you, Mr. James."

As Ryland shook his hand, he grinned. "Call me Ryland."

Connor's eyes widened. He looked almost giddy with excitement. "Okay, Ryland."

He motioned to the soccer ball. "Looks like you've been practicing. It's good to get some touches on the ball every day."

Connor nodded. The kid was totally starstruck. Lucy didn't blame him for being wowed by Ryland. She was, too.

Better be careful.

Ryland used his left foot to push the ball toward Connor. "Let's see you juggle."

Connor swooped up the ball and bounced it off his bony knees. He used his legs and feet to keep the ball from touching the ground.

"You're doing great," Ryland encouraged.

Connor beamed and kept going.

Ryland glanced at her. "He reminds me of Aaron."

"Two peas in a pod," she agreed.

The ball bounced away. Connor ran after it. "I'll try it again."

"The more you practice, the better you'll get," Ryland said.

"That's what Aunt Lucy told me."

His gaze met hers. Lucy's pulse skittered at the flirtatious gleam in Ryland's hazel eyes.

"Your aunt is a smart woman," he said.

Lucy didn't feel so smart. She wasn't sure what to make of her reaction to Ryland being here. Okay, the guy was handsome. Gorgeous, really. But she knew better than to be bowled over by a man and sweet talk.

So why was she practically swooning over the sexy soccer star? Ryland showing up and the way he was interacting with Connor had to be the reason. Nothing else made sense.

She straightened. "I thought you were going to call."

"I decided to stop by, instead."

Warning bells rang in her head. "The address isn't on my business card. How did you find this place?"

"I went into the café for a cup of coffee and asked where Aaron lived," Ryland explained. "Three people offered directions."

"That's Wicksburg for you," she said. "Friendly to a fault."

"No kidding," he agreed. "I received a friendly reminder about the difference between a tornado watch versus a tornado warning. More than one person also suggested I drop my dad's old truck off at the salvage yard before he gets home from vacation. But it's a good thing he has it. The truck is the only vehicle that has enough room so I can drive with my left foot."

"You went to so much trouble. A phone call would've been fine."

He motioned to her nephew. "Not for him."

A big grin brightened Connor's face. The heartache of the last few weeks seemed to have vanished. He looked happy and carefree, the way a nine-year-old boy should be.

Words didn't seem enough, but gratitude was all Lucy could afford to give Ryland. "Thank you."

"Watch this," Connor said.

"I'm watching," Ryland said, sounding amused.

Her nephew juggled the ball. His face, a portrait in concentration.

"Keep it going," Ryland encouraged.

"You're all he's talked about for the last two days," she said quietly. "I'm so happy you're here. I mean, Connor's happy. We're both happy."

"That makes three of us," Ryland said.

"Did you find a coach for the Defeeters?" Connor asked.

"Not a head coach, but someone who can help out for now."

"I knew it!" Connor screamed loud enough for the entire town to hear. The ball bounced into the hedge again.

Ryland had done his part, more than Lucy had expected. Warmth flowed through her. Not good. She shouldn't feel anything where he was concerned. She wanted him to give his talk to the team ASAP so she could say goodbye. "Thanks."

"So who's going to help coach us?" Connor asked eagerly.

Ryland smiled, a charming lopsided grin that made her remember the boy he used to be, the one she'd fallen head over heels for when she'd been a teenager.

"I am," he said.

CHAPTER FOUR

THE next week, on Monday afternoon, Ryland walked through the parking lot at Wicksburg Elementary School. Playing soccer here was one of the few good memories he had of the place.

He hoped today's soccer practice went well. He was looking forward to spending time with Lucy, and as for the boys... how hard could it be to coach a bunch of eight- and nine-year-olds?

Ryland adjusted the strap of the camp-chair bag resting on his left shoulder. He hated the idea of sitting during any portion of the practice, but standing for an entire hour wouldn't be good if his foot started hurting.

Healing was his number one priority. He had to be smart about helping the Defeeters. Not only because of his foot. His agent and the Fuego's front office might not consider a pseudo coaching gig "laying low." He'd sent an email to all the boys' parents explaining the importance of keeping his presence with the team quiet.

A car door slammed.

He glanced in the direction of the sound. Lucy's head appeared above the roof of a car.

Ryland hoped she was happier to see him today. The uncertainty in her eyes when he'd said he would help with the Defeeters had surprised him. When he explained no one else wanted to coach, so he'd decided to do it himself, a resigned smile settled on her lips. But she hadn't looked happy or relieved about the news.

He'd wanted a challenge. It appeared he'd gotten one.

She bent over, disappearing from his sight, then reappeared. Another door shut.

Her strawberry-blond curls bounced. His fingers itched to see if the strands felt as silky as they looked.

Lucy stepped out from between two cars with a bag of equipment in one hand and a binder in the other. She was alone.

He hoped her nephew wasn't sick. At least Lucy had shown up.

That made Ryland happy. So did the spring weather. He gave a quiet thanks for the warm temperature. Lucy had ditched the baggy hoodies she'd worn at his parents' house and at Aaron's. Her sweatshirts and pants had been hiding treasures.

Her outfit today showed off her figure to perfection. A green T-shirt stretched tight across her chest. Her breasts were round and high, in proportion and natural looking. Navy shorts accentuated the length of her legs. Firm and sexy. Ryland preferred the pale skin color to the orangey fake tan some women had.

Little Lucy Martin was a total hottie. Ryland grinned. Coaching the Defeeters was looking better and better.

Her gaze caught his. She pressed her lips together in a thin, tight line.

Busted. He'd been staring at her body. Practically leering. Guilt lodged in his throat.

A twinge of disappointment ran through him, too. Her reaction made one thing clear. She no longer had a crush on him.

He wasn't surprised. Crushes came and went. Over a decade had passed since they knew each other as kids. But Ryland didn't get why Lucy looked so unhappy to see him. If not for him, she would be on her own coaching the boys. He didn't expect her to fall at his feet, but a smile—even a hint of one— would have been nice.

She glanced toward the grass field.

He half expected her to walk away from him, but instead she headed toward him. Progress? He hoped so. "Hello."

"Hi," she said.

"Where's Connor?"

"He went home from school with a boy from the team. They should be here soon."

"A playdate and the first practice of spring. Connor is a lucky kid."

"I wanted to make today special for him."

"You have." Ryland liked how Lucy did so much for her nephew, but she seemed to give, give, give. He wondered if she ever did anything for herself. Maybe that was how he could get on her good side. "The first practice is always interesting. Getting to know a new coach. Sizing up who has improved over the break. Making friends with new teammates. At least that's how I remember it."

"All I know is Connor has been looking forward to this for weeks," she said. "He's been writing letters and sending emails to Aaron and Dana counting down the days to the start of practice, but they must be somewhere without computer access. They haven't replied the past couple of days."

That didn't sound good. "Worried?"

Lucy shrugged but couldn't hide the anxiousness in her eyes. "Aaron said this could happen. Connor just wants to hear what his dad thinks about you working with the team."

She hadn't answered Ryland's question about being worried, but he let it go. "I hope I live up to Connor's expectations."

"You really don't have to do this."

"I don't mind showing up early to practice."

"I was talking about coaching."

That wasn't what he'd expected her to say, but Lucy didn't seem to mince words. She also wore her heart on her sleeve. He didn't like seeing the tight lines around her mouth and narrowed eyes. He wanted to put her at ease. "It might be the last thing I expected to be doing while I'm in Wicksburg. But I want to do this for Aaron and his son."

For Lucy, too. But Ryland figured saying that would only upset her more.

"What if someone finds out?" she asked.

That thought had crossed his mind many times over the past

few days. Someone outside the team would recognize him at some point and most likely wouldn't be able to keep quiet.

But he was a man who took chances.

Besides how much trouble could he get into helping a bunch of kids? Community involvement was a good thing, surely? "I'll deal with that if it happens, but remember, I'm not coaching. I'm only helping."

A carefully laid out distinction that made a world of difference. At least he hoped so.

He waited for her to say something, to rattle off a list of reasons why his assisting the Defeeters was a bad idea or to tell him she'd found someone else to coach the team.

Instead, she raised the bag of equipment—balls and orange cones—in the air. "I picked up the practice gear. I also have a binder with emergency and player information."

Interesting. He'd expected her to put up more of a fight. He'd kind of been looking forward to it. When Lucy got emotional, silvery sparks flashed in her irises. He liked her blue eyes. And the rest of her, too. "Thanks."

"So what do you want to do with the cones?" she asked. "I've never been to a soccer practice before."

This was why Ryland wanted—no, needed—to help. He wouldn't be working only with the kids. He would be teaching Lucy what to do so she'd be all set when fall season rolled around. He didn't want the Defeeters split up as a team in September because they didn't have a coach for fall league. That wouldn't be good for the boys or for Aaron when he returned home. Lucy might end up feeling bad, too. "I'll show you."

With Lucy at his side, Ryland stepped from the asphalt onto the field. The smell of fresh grass filled his nostrils, the scent as intoxicating as a woman's perfume. He inhaled to take another sniff. Anticipation zinged through him, bringing all his nerve endings to life.

Neither soccer nor women had been part of his life since his foot surgery. He shot a sideward glance at Lucy. At least one of them would be now. Well, sort of.

"It's good to be back," he said, meaning it.

"In town?" she asked.

"On this field." For the last eleven years, no matter what level he played, soccer had meant packed stadiums, cheering crowds and vuvuzelas being blown. Shirtless men with painted faces and chests stood in the stands. Women with tight, tiny tops wanted body parts autographed. Smiling, he motioned to the field in front of him. "It doesn't matter whether I'm at an elementary school for a practice or at a sold-out stadium for a World Cup game. This is…home."

A dreamy expression formed on Lucy's face.

He stared captivated wondering what she was thinking about.

"I felt that way about this loft in Chicago." The tone of her voice matched the wistfulness in her eyes. "They rented studio space by the hour. The place smelled like paint and thinner, but that made it even more perfect. I couldn't afford to rent time that often, but when I did, I'd stay until the last second."

All the tension disappeared from around her mouth and forehead. Joy lit up her pretty face.

Warmth flowed though his veins. This was how Lucy should always look.

"Do you have a place to work on your art here?" he asked, his voice thick.

"No. It's just something I pursue in my spare time. I don't have much of that right now between Connor and my graphic-design business."

He didn't like how she brushed aside her art when talking about the studio loft made her so happy. "If you enjoy it…"

"I enjoy spending time with Connor." She glanced at her watch. "We should get ready for the boys to arrive."

Ryland would have rather found out more about her art and her. But he still had time.

"So the cones?" she asked again.

Her practical, down-to-business attitude didn't surprise him, but he was amused. He couldn't wait to break through her hard shell. "How do you think they should be set up?"

She raised her chin slightly. "You tell me. You're the coach."

"Officially, you are." Lucy had listed herself as the head coach with the league, which kept Ryland's name off the coach's list and league website. Besides, he wouldn't be here for the whole season. "I'm your helper."

"I may be listed as the head coach," she said. "But unofficially, as long as you're here to help, my most important job is to put together the snack list."

"That job is almost as important as coaching. Snacks after the game were my favorite part of rec. soccer."

Though now that Ryland had seen her go-on-forever legs, he might have to rethink that. A mole on the inside of her calf just above her ankle drew his attention. He wondered what her skin would taste like.

"Ryland…"

Lucy's voice startled him. He forced his gaze onto her face.

Annoyance filled her blue eyes, but no silver sparks flashed. "The cones."

Damn. He'd been caught staring twice now, but all her skin showing kept taking him by surprise. He wondered how she'd look in a bikini or…naked. Pretty good, he imagined. Though thinking about Lucy without any clothes on wasn't a smart idea. He needed to focus on the practice. "Two vertical lines with a horizontal connecting them at the top. Five cones on each side."

She dropped the equipment bag on the grass. "While I do that, set up your chair and take the weight off your foot. You don't want anything to slow down your recovery."

And your departure from town. The words may not have been spoken, but they were clearly implied.

Before he could say anything, she walked away, hips swaying, curls bouncing.

Too bad she was out-of-bounds.

Ryland removed his chair from the bag and opened it up. But he didn't sit. His foot didn't hurt.

He ran over the practice in his mind. His injury would keep him from teaching by example. He needed someone with two working feet to show the boys what needed to be done. Someone like…

"Lucy."

"Just a minute." She placed the last cone on the grass. "What do you need?"

You. Too bad that wasn't possible. But a brilliant albeit somewhat naughty idea formed in his mind. "I'm going to need you to show the boys what to do during warm-ups and drills."

Her eyes widened. "I've never done anything like this before. I have no idea what you want me to do."

Ryland wanted her. It was as simple as that. Or would be if circumstances were different. "I'll show you."

"O-kay."

Her lack of enthusiasm made him smile. "It's soccer not a walk down death row."

"Maybe not from your point of view," she said. "Show me."

"I want the boys to do a dynamic warm-up," he explained. "They'll break up into two groups. One half will go on the outside of the cones, the other half on the inside. Each time around they'll do something different to warm up their muscles."

"That sounds complicated."

"It's easy."

"Maybe for a pro soccer star."

Star, huh? He was surprised she thought of him that way. But he liked it. "Easy for a nine-year-old, too."

She followed him to the cones.

"The first lap I want you to jog around the outside of the cones."

"The boys know how to do that."

"I want them to see how to do it the right way."

Ryland watched her jog gracefully around the cones.

"Now what?" she asked.

"Backward."

She walked over to the starting point and went around the cones backward.

Each time he told her what to do, whether skipping and jumping at each cone or reaching down to pull up the toe of her tennis shoe. A charming pink colored her cheeks from her efforts. Her breasts jiggled from the movement.

This had to be one of his best ideas ever. Ryland grinned wickedly, pleased with himself. "Face the cones and shuffle sideward."

She did something that looked like a step from the Electric Slide or some other line dance popular at wedding receptions.

"Let me help you." He walked over, kneeled on his good leg and touched her left calf. The muscles tightened beneath his palms. But her skin felt as soft as it looked. Smooth, too. "Relax. I'm not going to hurt you."

"That's what they all say," she muttered.

Ryland had no idea what she meant or who "they all" might be, but he wanted to find out.

"Bring your foot to the other one, instead of crossing the leg behind." He raised her boot off the ground and brought it over to the other foot. "Like this."

Her cheeks reddened more. "You could have just told me."

He stood. "Yeah, but this way is more fun."

"Depends on your definition of fun."

Lucy shuffled around the cones.

Ryland enjoyed watching her. This was as close as he'd gotten to a female next to the housecleaner his mom had hired while she was away. Mrs. Henshaw was old enough to be his mother.

"Anything else?" Lucy asked when she'd finished.

There was more, but he didn't want to do too many new things at the first practice. Both for Lucy's and the boys' sakes.

"A few drills." The sound of boys' laughter drifted on the air. "I'll show you those when the time comes. The team is here."

"Nervous?"

"They're kids," Ryland said. "No reason to be nervous."

Lucy studied him. "Ever spend much time with eight- and nine-year-olds?"

Not unless you counted signing autographs, posing for photographs and walking into stadiums holding their hands. "No, but I was a kid once."

She raised an arched brow. "Once."

He winked.

Lucy smiled.

Something passed between them. Something unexpected and unwelcome. Uh-oh.

A loud burp erupted from behind them followed by laughter.

Whatever was happening with Lucy came to an abrupt end. Good, because whatever connection Ryland had felt with her wasn't something he wanted. Flirting was one thing, but this couldn't turn into a quick roll in the sheets. He couldn't afford to let that happen while he was here in Wicksburg. "The Defeeters have arrived."

Lucy looked toward the parking lot. "Aaron told me coaching this age is a lot like herding cats," Lucy explained. "Except that cats don't talk back."

Another burp sounded. More laughter followed.

"Or burp," Ryland said.

As she nodded, boys surrounded them. He'd played in big games in front of millions of people, but the expectant look in these kids' eyes disconcerted him, making him feel as if he was stepping onto the pitch for the very first time.

"Hey, boys. I'm Ryland." He focused on the eager faces staring up at him, not wanting to disappoint them or Lucy. "I'm going to help out for a few games. You boys ready to play some football?"

Nine—or was it ten?—heads, ranging in size and hair color, nodded enthusiastically.

Great. Ryland grinned. This wouldn't be difficult at all.

A short kid with long blond hair scrunched his nose. "This isn't football."

"Everywhere else in the world soccer is called football," Ryland explained.

The kid didn't look impressed. "It's called soccer here."

"We'll talk more about that later." Soccer in America was nothing like soccer in other parts of the world. No sport in the

U.S. could compare with the passion for the game elsewhere. "I want you to tell me your name and how long you've played."

Each boy did. Justin. Jacob. Dalton. Tyler. Marco. The names ran into each other. Ryland wasn't going to be able to remember them. No worries. Calling them dude, bud and kid would work for today. "Let's get working."

"Can you teach us how to dive?" a boy with beach-blond hair that hung over his eyes asked.

Some soccer players dived—throwing themselves on the field and pretending to be hurt—to draw a penalty during the game. "No," Ryland said firmly. "Never dive."

"What if it's the World Cup?" a kid with a crew cut asked.

"If you're playing in the World Cup, you'll know what to do." Ryland clapped his hands together. "Time to warm up."

The boys stood in place.

He knew the warm-up routine, and so did his Fuego teammates, but based on these kids' puzzled looks, they hadn't a clue what he was talking about. "Get in a single file line behind the first cone on the left side."

The boys shuffled into place, but it wasn't a straight line. Two kids elbowed each other as they jockeyed for the spot in front of Connor. A couple kids in the middle tried to trip each other. The boys in the back half didn't seem to understand the meaning of a line and spread out.

This wasn't working out the way he'd planned. Ryland dragged his hand through his hair.

"Meow," Lucy whispered.

"So where can I find a cat herder?" he asked.

Her coy smile sent his pulse racing. "Look in the mirror. Didn't you know cat herder is synonymous with coach?"

"That's what I was afraid you'd say."

The hour flew by. Lucy stood next to Ryland on a mini-field he'd had her set up using cones. She hadn't known what to expect with the boys' first practice, but she begrudgingly gave him credit. The guy could coach.

After a rocky start, he'd harnessed the boys' energy with

warm-up exercises and drills. He never once raised his voice. He didn't have to. His excitement about the game mesmerized both the boys and Lucy. Out on the field, he seemed larger-than-life, sexier, despite the boot on his foot. Thank goodness practice was only sixty minutes, twice a week. That was more than enough time in his presence. Maybe even too much.

Ryland focused on the boys, but her gaze kept straying to him. The man was so hot. She tried hard to remain unaffected. But it wasn't easy, especially when she couldn't forget how it felt when he'd moved her leg earlier.

Talk about being a hands-on coach. His touch had surprised her. But his tenderness guiding her leg had made her want... more.

And when he'd stood behind her, his hard body pressed against her backside, helping her figure out the drills so she could show the boys...

Lucy swallowed. More wasn't possible, no matter how appealing it might sound at the moment. Being physically close to a man had felt good. She'd forgotten how good that could be. But getting involved with a guy wasn't on her list of things to do. Not when she had Connor to take care of.

"Great pass, Tyler." Ryland turned to her. "Do you know if Aaron uses set plays?"

"I have no idea," she admitted. "I have his coaching notebook if you want to look through it."

"I would. Thanks."

"I should be thanking you," she said. "The boys have learned so much from you today. More than I could have taught them over an entire season."

"I appreciate that, but you'll be ready to do this when the time comes."

She doubted that.

All but two of the boys surrounded the ball.

Ryland grimaced.

Lucy appreciated how seriously he took practice, because she needed to figure out what should be happening on the field. "Something went wrong, but I have no idea what."

He pointed to the cluster of boys. "See how the players are gathered together and focused only on the ball?"

She nodded.

"They need to spread out and play their position." He pointed to the fastest kid on the team—Dalton. "All that kid wants is the ball. Instead of playing in the center, where he should be, he's back on the left side chasing down the ball and playing defender. See how that black-haired kid, Mason—"

"Marco," she corrected.

"Yeah, Marco," Ryland said. "You've got Marco and Dalton and those other players all in the same area."

Ryland's knowledge of the game impressed her. Okay, he was a professional soccer player. But he never stopped pointing things out to her and helping the boys improve. She should have brought a notebook and pen so she could write down everything he said. It was like being enrolled at Soccer University and this was Basic Ball Skills 101. She, however, didn't feel like she had the prerequisites to attend.

"So what do you do?" she asked.

Ryland raised the silver whistle around his neck. "This."

As he blew the whistle, she wondered what his lips would feel like against her skin. Probably as good as his hands. Maybe even better.

Stop thinking about it.

The boys froze.

"This isn't bunch ball," Ryland said. "Don't chase the ball. Spread out. Play your position. Try again."

The boys did.

Ryland directed them to keep them from bunching again. He clapped when they did something right and corrected them when they made mistakes.

As she watched Ryland coach, warmth pooled inside Lucy. She forced her gaze back on the boys.

The play on the field reminded her of an accordion. Sometimes the boys were spread out. Other times they came together around the ball.

"Will telling them fix the problem?" she asked.

"No. They're still very young. But they'll start realizing what they're supposed to do," he said. "Only practice and game time will make the lesson stick."

Lucy wondered if that was what it took to become a competent coach. She had a feeling she would be doing her best just to get by.

The energy on the field intensified. Connor passed the ball to Dalton who shot the ball over the goalie's head. Goal!

"Yes!" Ryland shouted. "That's how you do it."

The boys gave each other high fives.

"That score was made possible by Connor moving to a space. He has good instincts just like his dad." Ryland's smile crinkled the corners of his eyes.

Her pulse quickened. "Wish you could be out there playing?"

He shrugged. "I always want to play, but being here sure beats sitting on my dad's easy chair with a dog on my lap."

His comment about his dad made Lucy look toward the parking lot. A line of parents waited to pick up their boys. She glanced at her watch. Uh-oh. She'd lost track of the time. "Practice ended five minutes ago."

"That was fast." Ryland blew the whistle again. "I want everyone to jog around the field to cool down. Don't run, just a nice easy pace."

The boys took off, some faster than the others.

"The team did well," Ryland said to her.

"So did you."

He straightened. "This is different from what I'm used to."

"You rose to the occasion." Lucy couldn't have worked the boys like he had. She usually preferred doing things on her own. But she needed Ryland's help with the team. Thank goodness she'd listened to Connor and taken a chance by going to see Ryland. "I learned a lot. And the boys had fun."

"Soccer is all about having fun when you're eight and nine."

"What about when you're twenty-nine?" she asked, curious about his life back in Phoenix.

"There are some added pressures and demands, but no complaints," he said. "I'm living the dream."

"Not many can say that." She sure couldn't, but maybe someday. Nah, best not to get her hopes up only to be disappointed. "Aaron says you worked hard to get where you are."

"That's nice of him. But it's amazing what being motivated can do for a kid."

"You wanted to play professionally."

"I wanted to get out of Wicksburg," he admitted. "I didn't have good grades because I liked kicking a ball more than studying so that messed up any chance of getting a football scholarship."

Football? She was about to ask when she remembered what he'd said at the beginning of practice. Soccer was called football overseas. That was where he'd spent the majority of his career. "Small-town boy who made it big."

"That was the plan from the beginning."

His wide smile sent her heart beating triple time. Lucy didn't understand her response. "I'd say you succeeded splendidly."

Whereas she... Lucy didn't want to go there. But she knew someone successful like Ryland would never be satisfied living in a small, boring town like Wicksburg. He must be counting the weeks, maybe even the days, until he could escape back to the big city. While she would remain here as long as she was needed.

As the boys jogged toward them, Ryland gave each one a high five. "Nice work out there. Practice your juggling at home. Learning to control the ball will make you a better player. Now gather up the cones and balls so we can get out of here. I don't know about you, but I'm hungry."

The boys scattered in search of balls like mice looking for bits of cheese. They dribbled the balls back. Lucy placed them inside the mesh bag. The boys picked up their water bottles then walked off the field to their parents.

Connor's megawatt smile could light up half of Indiana. "That was so much fun."

"You played hard out there," Ryland said.

Her nephew shot her a quick glance. "All that running made me hungry, too."

"I've got dinner in the slow cooker," Lucy said.

"Want to eat with us, Ryland?" Connor asked. "Aunt Lucy always makes enough food so we can have leftovers."

Spending more time with Ryland seemed like a bad idea, but she was more concerned about Connor. She couldn't always shield him from disappointment, but with him adjusting to his parents being away, she wanted to limit it. "That's nice of you to think of Ryland. We have enough food to share, but I'm sure he has somewhere else to be tonight."

There, she'd given Ryland an easy out from the dinner invitation. No one's feelings would be hurt.

"I'm free tonight," he said to her dismay. "But I wouldn't want to intrude."

"You're not." Connor looked at Lucy for verification.

She was still stuck on Ryland being free tonight. She figured he would have a date, maybe two, lined up. Unless he had a girlfriend back in Phoenix.

"Tell him it's okay, Aunt Lucy." Her nephew was using his lost puppy-dog look to his full advantage. "Ryland's coaching the team. The least we can do is feed him."

"You sound like your mom." Lucy's resolve weakened. "She's always trying to feed everyone."

Connor nodded. "That's how we ended up with Manny. Mom kept putting tuna out for him. One day he came inside and never left."

Ryland smiled. "He sounds like a smart cat."

"We call him Manny, but his full name is Manchester," Connor said.

Amusement filled Ryland's eyes. "After the Red Devils."

Connor nodded. "Man U rules."

"If Manny was a girl, I'm guessing you wouldn't have named her Chelsea."

Connor looked aghast. "Never."

Ryland grinned. "At least I know where your loyalties lie."

"I have no idea what you're talking about," Lucy admitted.

"Manchester United and Chelsea are teams in the Premier League in England," Ryland explained.

"Rivals," Connor added. "Can Ryland come over, please?"

Lucy could rattle off ten reasons not to have him over, but she had a bigger reason to say yes—Connor.

"You're welcome to join us." If Lucy didn't agree, she would never hear the end of it from her nephew. Besides, she liked how he smiled whenever Ryland was around. It was one meal. No big deal. "We have plenty of food."

"Thanks," he said. "I'm getting tired of grilling."

Connor's eyes widened. "You cook?"

"If I don't cook, I don't eat," Ryland explained. "When I moved to England, I had to cook, clean and do my own laundry. Just like my mom made me do when I was growing up."

His words surprised Lucy. She would have expected a big-shot soccer star to have a personal chef or eat out all the time, not be self-sufficient around the house. Her Jeff, her ex-husband, did nothing when it came to domestic chores.

"I'll have to learn how to do those things," Connor said with a serious expression.

"You're on your way," Ryland encouraged. "You already make great chocolate-chip cookies."

Connor's thin chest puffed slightly. "Yeah, I do."

Lucy shook her head. "You're supposed to say thank you when someone compliments you."

"Even if it's true?" Connor asked.

Ryland's smiled widened. "Especially then."

Connor shrugged. "Okay. Thank you."

Having Ryland over was exactly what Connor needed. But a part of her wondered if it was what she needed, too.

Now that was silly.

Ryland was coming over for dinner because of her nephew. Just because she might like the idea of being around him a little longer didn't mean anything at all.

CHAPTER FIVE

IN THE kitchen, the smell of spices, vegetables and beef simmering in the slow cooker lingered in the air. The scents brought back fond memories of family dinners with Aaron and her parents. But other than the smell, tonight wasn't going to be as comfortable as any of those dinners growing up.

Lucy checked the oven. Almost preheated to the correct temperature.

Ryland had heated her up earlier. She couldn't stop thinking about how he'd touched her at practice. His large, warm hand against her skin. Leaning against the counter, she sighed.

The guy really was…

She bolted upright.

Lucy needed to stop fantasizing and finish making dinner. She was a divorced twenty-six-year-old, not a swooning teenager. She knew better than to be crushing on any man, let alone Ryland James. The guy could charm the pants off everybody. Well, everyone except for her.

She placed the uncooked biscuits on a cookie sheet.

The sounds of laser beams from a video game and laughter from all the fun drifted into the kitchen. Ryland's laugh was deep and rich, thick and smooth, like melted dark chocolate.

Lucy opened the oven door and slid the tray of biscuits onto the middle rack. Would he taste as good as he sounded?

The pan clattered against the back of the oven.

"Need help?" Ryland yelled from the living room.

Annoyed at herself for thinking about *him* that way when

she knew better, she straightened the pan then closed the oven door. "Everything's fine."

Or would be when he was gone.

Okay, that wasn't fair. Connor was laughing and having fun. Her nephew needed Ryland, so did the team. That meant she needed him, too.

Watching a couple of videos and reading some books weren't the same as having Ryland show her what needed to be done at practice. The boys would have been the ones to suffer because of her cluelessness. Feeding Ryland dinner was the least she could do to repay him. It wasn't as if she'd had to go to any extra trouble preparing the meal.

Nor was it Ryland's fault he was gorgeous and seemed to press every single one of her buttons. Being around him reminded her that a few of the male species had redeeming qualities. Ones like killer smiles, sparkling eyes, enticing muscles, warm hands and a way with kids. But she knew better than to let herself get carried away.

"I'm going to win," Connor shouted with glee.

"Not so fast," Ryland countered. "I'm not dead yet."

"Just you wait."

The challenge in her nephew's voice loosened her tight shoulder muscles. Boys needed a male influence in their lives. Even if that influence filled her stomach with butterflies whenever he was nearby.

No worries, Lucy told herself. She hadn't been around men for a while. That had to be the reason for her reaction to Ryland.

She tossed the salad. The oven timer buzzed.

With the food on the table, she stood in the doorway to the kitchen with a container of milk in one hand and a pitcher of iced tea in the other. "Dinner's ready."

Connor took his normal seat. He pointed to a chair across, the one next to where Lucy had been sitting since she arrived a month ago. The "guest spots" at the table. "Sit there, Ryland. The other chairs are my mom's and dad's."

Ryland sat. The table seemed smaller with him there, even though it seated six.

Ignoring her unease, Lucy filled everyone's glasses. She sat, conscious of him next to her.

Her leg brushed his. Lucy stiffened. The butterflies in her stomach flapped furiously. She tucked her feet beneath her chair to keep from touching Ryland again. Next time...

There wouldn't be a next time.

Her nephew grabbed two biscuits off the plate. "These are my favorite."

Ryland took one. "Everything smells delicious."

The compliment made Lucy straighten. She hadn't cooked much after the divorce so felt out of practice. But Connor needed healthy meals so she was getting back in the habit. "Thanks."

As she dished up the stew, Ryland filled his salad plate using a pair of silver tongs. His arm brushed hers. Heat emanated from the spot of contact. "Excuse me."

"That's okay." But the tingles shooting up her arm weren't. Lucy hated the way her body reacted to even the slightest contact with him. She pressed her elbows against her side. No more touching.

Flatware clinked against bowls and plates. Ryland and Connor discussed the upcoming MLS season. She recognized some of the team names, but nothing else.

"Who's your favorite team?" Ryland asked her.

She moved a carrot around with her fork. Stew was one of her favorite dishes, but she wasn't hungry. Her lack of appetite occurred at the same time as Ryland's arrival at the house. "The only soccer games I watch are Connor's."

"That was when you lived here with Uncle Jeff," Connor said. "After you moved away you didn't come to any."

"That's true." Curiosity gleamed in Ryland's eyes, but she ignored it. She didn't want to discuss her ex-husband over dinner or in front of Connor. No matter how badly Jeff had betrayed her and their marriage vows, he'd been a good uncle and still sent Connor birthday and Christmas presents. "But I'll get to see all your games now."

Lucy reached for the salt. Extra seasoning might make the

stew more appealing. She needed to eat something or she'd find herself starving later. That had happened a lot when she moved to Chicago. She didn't want a repeat performance here.

Ryland's hand covered hers around the saltshaker.

She stiffened.

He smiled. "Great minds think alike."

Too bad she couldn't think. Not with his large, warm hand on top of hers.

Darn the man. Ryland must know he was hot stuff. But he'd better think twice before he put any moves on her. She pulled her hand away, leaving the salt for him.

Ryland handed the shaker to her. "You had it first."

Lucy added salt to her stew. "Thanks."

"I forgot to tell you, Aunt Lucy. Tyler got a puppy," Connor said, animated. "His parents took him to the animal shelter, and Tyler got to pick the dog out himself." Connor relayed the entire story, including how the dog went potty on the floor in the kitchen as soon as they arrived home. "I bet Manny would like to have a dog. That way he'd never be lonely."

Oh, no. Lucy knew exactly where her nephew was going with this. Connor had used a similar tactic to get her to buy him a new video game. But buying an inanimate object was different than a living, breathing puppy.

"Manny is rarely alone." She passed the saltshaker to Ryland. "I work from home."

Connor's forehead wrinkled, as if he were surprised she hadn't said yes right away. "But you don't chase him around the house. When I'm at school he just lays around and sleeps."

Ryland feigned shock. "You don't chase Manny?"

Lucy wanted to chase Ryland out of here. She hated how aware she was of him. Her blood simmered. She drank some iced tea, but that didn't cool her down. "Cats lay around and sleep. That's what they like to do during the day. I don't think Manny is going to be too keen on being chased by a dog. He's not a kitten anymore."

"Don't forget. Dogs make big messes outside," Ryland said. "You're going to have to clean it all up with a shovel or rake."

Connor scrunched his face. "I'm going to have to scoop up the poop?"

Okay, maybe having Ryland here wasn't so bad. She appreciated how skillfully he'd added a dose of dog-care reality to the conversation. He might make her a little hot and bothered, but he'd saved her a lot of back and forth by bringing up the mess dogs left in the yard. A fair trade-off in the grand scheme of things. At least she hoped so.

"Yes, you would have to do that." No matter how badly Connor wanted a puppy she couldn't make that decision without Aaron and Dana. Getting a pet wasn't a commitment to make lightly. "A dog is something your parents have to decide on, not me. Owning a dog is a big responsibility."

"Huge," Ryland agreed, much to Lucy's relief. "I've been taking care of my parents' dog Cupcake. I never knew something so little would take so much work. She either wants food or attention or to go outside on a walk."

"I've never taken a dog on a walk," Connor said.

"Maybe you could take Cupcake for a walk for me," Ryland suggested.

Connor nodded enthusiastically. "If it's okay with Aunt Lucy."

The longing in his blue eyes tugged at her heart. She couldn't say no to this request, even if it meant seeing Ryland outside of soccer again. "I'm sure we can figure out a time to take Cupcake for a walk."

"You can get a glimpse of what having a dog is like," Ryland said. "It might also be a good idea to see what Manny thinks of Cupcake. Cats and dogs don't always get along."

His words were exactly what a nine-year-old dog-wannabe owner needed to hear. The guy was turning into a knight in a shining soccer jersey. She would owe him dozens of chocolate-chip cookies for all he was doing for Connor.

Ryland smiled at her.

A feeling of warmth traveled from the top of her head to the tips of her toes. She'd better be careful or she was going to turn into a pile of goo. That would not be good.

"Did you ever have a dog?" Connor asked her.

"No, but we had cats and a few other animals," she replied. "Fish, a bird and reptiles."

As Ryland set his iced tea on the table, she bit into a biscuit. "Has your aunt told you about Squiggy?"

Lucy choked on the bread. She coughed and swallowed. "You remember Squiggy?"

Mischief danced in his eyes. "It's a little hard to forget being asked to be dig a grave and then rob it on the same day."

Connor's mouth formed a perfect O. "You robbed a grave?"

"Your dad and I did," Ryland said. "It was Squiggy's grave."

Connor leaned forward. "Who's Squiggy?"

Ryland winked at her.

Oh, no. He wouldn't tell… Who was she kidding? The mischievous gleam in his eyes was a dead giveaway he would spill every last detail. Might as well get it over with.

"Squiggy was my turtle. He was actually a tortoise," she explained. "But Squiggy was…"

"The best turtle in the galaxy," Ryland finished for her. "The fastest, too."

Lucy stared at him in disbelief. Those were the exact words she used to say to anyone who asked about her Squiggy. Other kids wanted dogs. She loved her hard-shelled, wrinkled reptile. "I can't believe you remember that."

"I told you I remembered a lot of stuff."

He had, but she thought Ryland was talking about when she'd been a teenager and sick. Not a seven-year-old girl who'd thought the sun rose and set on a beloved turtle.

"Your aunt doted on Squiggy," Ryland said. "Even painted his shell."

Lucy grinned. "Polka dots."

He nodded. "I recall pink and purple strips."

Memories rushed back like water over Cataract Falls on Mill Creek. "I'd forgotten about those."

"Your aunt used to hand-feed him lettuce. Took him on walks, too."

She nodded. "Squiggy might have been the fastest turtle around, but those walks still took forever."

"You never went very far," Ryland said.

"No, we didn't," she admitted. "Wait a minute. How did you know that?"

His smile softened. "Your mom had us watch you."

Her mother, make that her entire family, had always been so overprotective. Lucy had no idea they'd dragged Ryland into it, too. "And you guys accused me of following you around."

"You did follow us."

"Okay, I did, but that's what little sisters do."

Connor reached for his milk glass. "I wouldn't want a little sister."

"I never had a little sister," Ryland said. "But it felt like I had one with Lucy spying on us all the time."

She stuck her tongue out at him.

He did the same back to her.

Connor giggled.

Sitting here with Ryland brought back so many memories. When she was younger, she used to talk to him whenever he was over at the house with Aaron. Puberty and her crush had changed that. The awkward, horrible time of hormones and illness were all she'd remembered. Until now.

"Why did you have to rob Squiggy's grave?" Connor asked him.

Ryland stared into her eyes. His warm hazel gaze seemed to pierce through her. Breaking contact was the smart thing to do, but Lucy didn't want to look away.

For old times' sake, she told herself.

A voice inside her head laughed at the reasoning. A part of her didn't care. Looking was safe. It was all the other stuff that was…dangerous.

"Do you want to tell him or should I?" Ryland asked.

Emotion swirled inside her. Most of it had to do with the uncertainty she felt around him, not the story about her turtle. "Go ahead. I'm curious to hear your side of the story."

"I want to hear both sides," Connor announced.

"You will, if Ryland gets it wrong," she teased.

"I have a feeling you may be surprised," Ryland said.

She had a feeling he was right.

"Your aunt came to your dad and me with big crocodile tears streaming down her cheeks," Ryland explained. "She held a shoebox and said her beloved Squiggy had died. She wanted us to dig a hole so she could bury him."

"Before you go any further, I wanted to have a funeral, not just bury him. I would also like to remind Connor that I was only seven at the time."

Amusement gleamed in Ryland's eyes. "Age duly noted."

Connor inched forward on his chair. "What happened?"

"Your dad and I dug a hole. A grave for Squiggy's coffin."

"Shoebox," Lucy clarified.

Ryland nodded. "She placed the shoebox into the hole and tossed wilted dandelions on top of it. While your dad and I refilled the hole with dirt, your aunt Lucy played 'Taps' on a harmonica."

"Kazoo," she corrected. Still she couldn't believe all he remembered after so many years.

"A few words were spoken."

"From my favorite book at the time *Franklin in the Dark,*" she said.

"Who is Franklin?" Connor asked.

"A turtle from a series of children's books," Lucy explained. "It was turned into a cartoon that was shown on television."

"Aaron said a brief prayer," Ryland said. "Then your aunt stuck a tombstone made of Popsicle sticks into the ground and sprinkled more dandelions over the mound of dirt."

Lucy nodded. "It was a lovely funeral."

"Yeah," Ryland said. "Until you told us that Squiggy wasn't actually dead, and we had to unbury him so he wouldn't die."

Connor stared at her as if she were a short, green extra-terrestrial with laser beams for eyes. "You think some video games are too violent and you buried a live turtle?"

She squirmed under his intense scrutiny. "Some games

aren't appropriate for nine-year-olds. And nothing bad happened to Squiggy."

Fortunately. What had she been thinking? Maybe burying Barbie dolls had gotten too boring.

Ryland grinned. "But it was a race against time."

She had to laugh. "They dug so fast dirt flew everywhere."

"Aaron and I were sure we would be blamed if Squiggy died."

As her gaze collided with Ryland's again, something passed between them. A shared memory, she rationalized. That was all it could be. She looked at her untouched food. "But your dad and Ryland didn't get in trouble. They saved Squiggy."

Connor leaned over the table. "Squiggy didn't die under all that dirt?"

Ryland raised his glass. "Nope. Squiggy was alive and moving as slow as ever."

But that was the last time she'd thrown a funeral for anything living or inanimate. Her parents had made sure of that.

"So why did you bury him and have a funeral?" Connor asked.

Lucy knew this question would be coming once more of the story came out. "You know how some kids play house or restaurant?"

"Or army," Connor suggested.

She nodded. "One of the games I played was funeral."

"That's weird." Connor took another biscuit from the plate. "In school Mrs. Wilson told us turtles live longer than we do. Whatever happened to Squiggy?"

"He ran away," Lucy said. "Your dad and I grew up in a house that was near the park with that nice lake. We'd see turtles on tree trunks at the water's edge. Your dad told me Squiggy was lonely and ran away to live with the other turtles. I was sad and missed him so much, but your dad said I should be happy because Squiggy wanted to be in the park."

A beat passed. And another. Connor looked at Ryland. "So what really happened to Squiggy?"

Her mouth gaped.

A sheepish expression crossed Ryland's face.

Realization dawned. "Squiggy didn't run away."

Connor gasped. "Squiggy died!"

Ryland nodded once, but his gaze never left hers. "I thought you'd figured out what happened."

She'd been so quick to believe Aaron... Of course she'd wanted to believe it. "I never thought something bad might have happened to Squiggy."

"I'm sorry." The sincerity in Ryland's voice rang clear, but the knowledge still stung. "Aaron didn't want to put you through a real funeral because he knew how much Squiggy meant to you so we buried him one night in the park after you went to bed."

Lucy had imagined the adventures Squiggy had experienced at the pond. But the lie didn't surprise her. Few told her the truth once she'd gotten sick. It must have been the same way before she was so ill. "I should have figured that out."

"You were young," Ryland said. "There's nothing wrong with believing something if it makes us happy."

"Even if it's a lie?" she asked.

"A white lie so you wouldn't hurt so badly," he countered. "You know Aaron always watched out for you back then."

That much was true. Lucy nodded.

"My dad told me it's important to look out for others, especially girls." Connor scrunched his nose as if that last word smelled bad.

"He's right," Ryland said. "That's what your dad was doing with your aunt when Squiggy died. It's what he always did and probably still does with her and your mom."

Connor sat taller. "I'll have to do the same."

Ryland looked as proud of her nephew as she felt. "We all should," he said.

Her heart thudded. The guy was a charmer, but he sounded genuine.

But then so had Jeff, she reminded herself.

The harsh reality clarified the situation. She needed to rein in her emotions ASAP. Thinking of Ryland as anything other than the Defeeters' coaching assistant was not only dangerous but also stupid. She wasn't about to risk her heart with someone like that again.

She scooted back in her chair. "Who's ready for dessert?"

While Lucy tucked Connor back into bed, Ryland stared at the framed photographs setting on the fireplace mantel. Each picture showed a different stage in Aaron's life—army, marriage, family, college graduation. Those things were as foreign to Ryland as a three-hundred-pound American football linebacker trying to tackle him as he ran toward the goal.

Footsteps sounded behind him. "I think Connor's down for the count this time," Lucy said.

Finally. The kid was cool and knew a lot about soccer, but he hadn't left them alone all evening. Twice now Connor had gotten out of bed after they'd said good-night. "Third time's the charm."

"I hope so."

Ryland did, too. A repeat performance of today's practice with some touching would be nice, especially if she touched back. Having a little fun wouldn't hurt anyone. No one, not Mr. McElroy or Blake or Ryland's mom, would have to know what went on here tonight.

She sat on the couch. "Looking at Aaron's pictures?"

"Yeah." Ryland ran his fingertip along the top of a black wood frame, containing a picture of Aaron and Connor fishing. That was something fathers and sons did in Wicksburg. "Aaron's looks haven't changed that much, but he seems like quite the family guy."

Many professional players had a wife, kids and pets. When Ryland first started playing overseas, he hadn't wanted to let anything get in the way of his new soccer career and making a name for himself. He'd been a young, hungry hotshot.

Wait a minute. He still was. Only maybe not quite so young...

"It's hard to believe Aaron's only thirty. He's done a lot for his age," Lucy said with a touch of envy in her voice. "You both have."

Ryland shrugged. "I'm a year younger and have four, maybe five, years left to play if I'm lucky."

"That's not long."

Teams used up and threw away players. But he wasn't ready for that to happen to him. He also didn't want to hang on past his time and be relegated to a few minutes of playing time or be on a team in a lower league. "That's why I want to make the most of the time I have left in the game."

"Soccer is your priority."

"It's my life." He stared at Aaron's wedding picture. Knowing someone was there to come home to must be nice, but he'd made the decision not to divide his focus. Soccer was it. Sometimes Ryland felt a sense of loneliness even when surrounded by people. But occasionally feeling lonely wasn't a reason to get involved in a serious relationship. "That's why I won't start thinking about settling down until my career is over with."

"Playing the field might be hard to give up," she commented.

"Is that the voice of experience talking?"

"Someone I knew," she said. "That's not my type of...game."

A picture of Aaron wearing fatigues and holding a big rifle caught Ryland's attention. His old friend might consider him a foe for putting the moves on Lucy. He nudged the frame so the photo of Aaron looking big, strong and armed didn't directly face the couch.

Ryland flashed her his most charming smile. "What kind of games do you play?"

"None."

He strode to the couch. "That doesn't sound like much fun."

She shrugged. "Fun is in the eye of the beholder."

Holding her would be fun. He sat next to her.

Lucy smelled like strawberries and sunshine. Appealing and intoxicating like sweet ambrosia. He wouldn't mind a taste. But she seemed a little tense. He wanted the lines creasing her forehead to disappear so they could get comfortable and cozy. "I see lots of family photographs. Is any of your artwork here?"

"Yes."

"Show me something."

Her eyes narrowed suspiciously. "Are you asking to see my etchings?"

"I was thinking more along the lines of sketches and paintings, but if you have etchings and they happened to be in your bedroom…" he half joked.

She glanced toward the hallway he assumed led to the bedrooms. Interest twinkled in her eyes. Her pursed lips seemed to be begging for kisses. Maybe Lucy was more game than she let on.

Anticipation buzzed through him. All he needed was a sign from her to make his move. Unless she took the initiative. Now that would be a real turn-on.

Her gaze met his. "Not tonight."

Bummer. He didn't think she was playing hard to get so he had to take her words at face value. "Another time, maybe."

"I'll…see."

Her response didn't sound promising. That…bugged him. Some women would be all over him, trying to get him to kiss, touch, undress them. Lucy wanted nothing to do with him. At least outside of soccer practice.

Calling it a night would be his best move. A challenge was one thing, but there was no sense beating his head against the goalpost. He wasn't supposed to be flirting let alone wanting to kiss her. Too bad he didn't want to leave yet. "Anything I can do to help my cause?"

Her blue-eyed gaze watched him intently. "Not tonight."

Same answer as before. At least she was consistent.

Ryland stood. "It's getting late. Cupcake's been out in the dog run since before practice. She has a cushy doghouse, but she's going to be wondering where I've been. Thanks for dinner. A home-cooked meal was the last thing I was expecting tonight."

Lucy rose. "I wasn't expecting a dinner guest."

Ryland wished tonight could be ending differently, but he liked that she was honest and up-front. "We're even."

"I'd say your helping with the team outweighs my cooking dinner."

He wasn't quite ready to give up. "You could always invite me over for more meals."

Lucy raised an eyebrow. "Taking another shot?"

"Habit." A bad one under the circumstances. Not many would call him a gentleman, but Lucy deserved his respect. "Which means it's time for me to go. Practice is at five o'clock on Wednesday, right?"

She nodded.

He took a step toward the door. "See you then."

"Ryland…"

As he looked at her, she bit her lower lip. He would like to nibble on her lip. Yeah, right. He wanted to kiss her until she couldn't breathe and was begging for more.

Not tonight.

"Thanks," she said. "For coaching. I mean, helping out with the team. And being so nice to Connor."

Her warm eyes were as appealing as her mouth. "Your nephew is a great kid."

She nodded. "Having you here is just what we…he needed."

Ryland found her slip of the tongue interesting. Maybe she wasn't as disinterested as she claimed to be. He hoped she changed whatever opinion of him was holding her back. Earning her respect ranked right up there with tasting her kisses. "Anytime."

That was often a throwaway line, but he meant it with her.

Time to get the hell out of here before he said or did anything he might regret.

Lucy was the kind of woman you took home to meet your mother. The kind of woman who dreamed of a big wedding, a house with a white picket fence and a minivan full of kids. The kind of woman he normally avoided.

Best to leave before things got complicated. His life was far from perfect with all the demands and pressures on him, unwanted media attention and isolation, but his career was on the line. What was left of it, anyway. His reputation, too.

No woman was worth messing up his life for, not even the appealing, challenging and oh-so-enticing Lucy Martin.

CHAPTER SIX

ON WEDNESDAY afternoon, Lucy shaded an area on her sketch pad. The rapid movement of her pencil matched the way she felt. Agitated. Unnerved.

She'd filled half a sketch pad with drawings these past two days. An amazing feat considering she hadn't done any art since she'd left Chicago to return to Wicksburg. But she'd had to do something to take her mind off Ryland.

She took a closer look at the sketch. It was *him*. Again. If she wasn't thinking about Ryland, she was drawing him.

Lucy moved her pencil over the paper. She lengthened a few eyelashes. Women would kill for thick, luscious lashes like his. Heaven knew a tube of mascara couldn't come close to making her eyes look like that. So not fair.

Lucy shaded under his chin then raised her pencil.

Gorgeous.

Not the drawing, the man. The strength of his jaw, the flirtatious gleam in his eyes, his kissable lips.

Attraction heated her blood. What in the world was she doing drawing Ryland this way?

And then she realized…

She had another crush. But this felt different from when she'd been a teenager crushing on Ryland, stronger even than when she'd started dating her ex-husband.

Stupid.

Lucy closed the cover of her sketch pad, but every line,

curve and shadow of Ryland's face was etched on her brain. She massaged her aching temples.

Connor ran from the hallway to the living room. "I'm ready for practice."

He wore his soccer clothes—blue shirt, shorts and socks with shin guards underneath. As the shoelaces from his cleats dragged on the ground, he bounced from foot to foot with excitement.

Soccer practice was the last place she wanted to go. The less time she spent with Ryland, the better. She was too old to be feeling this way about him. About any guy. But skipping out wasn't an option. She was the head coach, after all. "Let me get my purse."

On the drive, Lucy glanced in the rearview mirror. Connor sat in the backseat, his shoulders hunched, as he played a game on his DS console. He was allowed a certain amount of videogame time each day, and he liked playing in the car. At least that kept him from talking about Ryland. Connor had a serious case of hero worship.

But that didn't mean she had to have one, too. Ryland hadn't known about her crush before. He didn't need to know about this one.

She would stay focused on soccer practice. No staring, admiring or lusting. No allowing Connor to invite him over for dinner tonight, either.

With her resolve firmly in place, Lucy parked then removed the soccer gear from her trunk. As Connor ran ahead of her, she noticed Ryland, dressed in his usual attire of shorts and a T-shirt, talking with Dalton's mom, Cheryl.

Lucy did a double take. Cheryl wore a tight, short skirt and a camisole. The clothing clung to every curve, showing lots of tanned skin and leaving little to the imagination. Not that Ryland would have to wait long to sample Cheryl's wares. She stood so close to him her large chest almost touched him.

Lucy gripped the ball bag in her hand.

Ryland didn't seem to mind. He stood his ground, not trying to put any distance between them.

Okay, maybe they weren't standing that close, but still...

Emotions swirled through her. She forced herself to look away.

No reason to be upset or jealous. She'd had her chance Monday night, but turned him down. Oh, she'd been tempted to have him stay and get comfy on the couch, but she was so thankful common sense had won over raging hormones. Especially now that he'd moved on to someone more...willing.

No worries. What two consenting adults did was none of her business. But like a moth drawn to a flame, she glanced over at them. She'd never considered herself masochistic, but she couldn't help herself.

Cheryl batted her mascara-laden eyelashes at him.

Ryland's grin widened. He'd used that same charming smile on Lucy after Connor had gone to bed.

Her stomach churned. Maybe she shouldn't have eaten the egg-salad sandwich for lunch. Maybe she needed to chill.

She quickened her pace. Not that either would notice her. They were too engrossed with each other.

No big deal. Ryland was a big boy, a professional athlete. He knew what he was getting into. He must deal with women hitting on him on a daily basis, ones who wouldn't think of telling him *not tonight.*

As she passed the two, Lucy focused on the boys. Seven of them stood in a circle and kicked the ball to one another while Marco ran around the center trying to steal the ball away.

Cheryl laughed, a nails-on-chalkboard sound that would make Cupcake howl. Lucy grimaced. If Ryland wanted to be with that kind of woman, he'd never be satisfied with someone like her. Not that she wanted to be with him.

Stop thinking about it! About him!

But she couldn't. No doubt this was some lingering reaction to Jeff's cheating. She'd thought it was great how her husband and her best friend since junior high, Amelia, got along. Lucy hadn't even suspected the two had been having an affair.

Better off without him. Without any of them. Men and best friends.

"Lucy."

Gritting her teeth, she glanced over her shoulder. Ryland was walking toward her. She waited for him. Even with the boot on his injured right foot, he moved with the grace of a world-class athlete, but looked more like a model for a sportswear company.

She didn't want to be impressed, but she couldn't blame Cheryl for wanting to get to know Ryland better. The guy was hot.

Maybe if Lucy hadn't taken a hiatus—more like a sabbatical—from men...

No. Even if she decided to jump back into the dating scene, he wasn't the right man for her. He wasn't the kind of guy to settle down let alone stick around. A superstar like Ryland James had too many women who wanted to be with him and would do anything to get close to him. He'd admitted he wouldn't start thinking about settling down until his career was over with. Why should he? Ryland had no reason to tie himself to only one woman and fight temptation on a daily basis.

Or worse, give in to it as Jeff had.

Ryland was smart for staying single and enjoying the... benefits that came with being a professional athlete.

He stopped next to her. "You sped by so fast I thought we were late starting practice."

He'd noticed her? With sexy Cheryl right there? Lucy was so stunned she almost missed the little thrill shooting through her. "I like being punctual."

The words sounded stupid as soon as she'd spoken them. She did like being on time, but that wasn't the reason she'd rushed by him. Telling him she'd been jealous of Cheryl wasn't happening. Not in this lifetime. She didn't need to boost his ego and decimate hers in one breath.

Ryland pulled out his cell phone and checked the time. He glanced at the boys on the field. "Practice doesn't start for ten minutes. We're still missing players."

Lucy noticed he didn't wear a watch or jewelry. She liked

that he didn't flaunt his wealth by wearing bling as some athletes she'd seen on television did.

Not that she cared what he wore.

Feeling flustered, she set the equipment bag on the grass.
"That'll give me plenty of time to set up."

His assessing gaze made Lucy feel as if she were an abstract
piece of art that he couldn't decide was valuable or not. She
didn't like it. If he was looking for a list of her faults, she could
give him one. Jeff had made it clear where she didn't stack up
in the wife department.

She placed her hands on her hips. "What?"

"You okay?" Ryland asked.

"Fine." The word came out quick and sharp. "Just one of
those days," she added.

Two more women, Suzy and Debbie, joined Cheryl. Both
wore the typical soccer-mom uniform—black track pants and
T-shirts. The women waved at Ryland. He nodded in their direction before turning his attention back to Lucy.

"Anything I can do to help?" he offered.

"You've done enough." She realized how that might sound.
She shouldn't be taking her feelings out on him. Like it or not,
she needed his help if she was going to learn enough about soccer to be helpful to the boys. Not just for the spring season, but
fall if no one else stepped up to coach. "I mean, you're doing
enough with the team. And Connor."

"I'm happy to do more for the boys and for you."

She should be grateful, but his offer irritated Lucy. She liked
being self-sufficient. Competent. Independent. Yet she was
having to depend on Ryland to help with the team, to teach her
about soccer and to keep a smile on Connor's face. She felt like
a failure...again. No way could she have him do more. "Let's
get set up so we can start on time."

As she removed the cones from the bag, she glanced up at
him.

Ryland stood watching her. With the sun behind him, he
looked almost angelic except the look in his eyes made her feel
as if he wanted to score with her, not the ball.

Lucy's heart lurched. Heat pooled within her. Common sense told her to ignore him and the hunger in his eyes. But she couldn't deny he made her feel sexy and desired. If only...

Stop. Now.

He was charming, handsome, and completely out of her league. An unexpected crush was one thing. It couldn't go any further than that.

"I can put them out," Ryland said.

No. Lucy didn't want any more help from him. She lowered her gaze to his mouth. His lips curved into a smile. Tingles filled her stomach.

And no matter how curious she might get or how flirtatious he might be, she didn't want any kisses from him, either. "Thanks, but I've got it."

A week later, Ryland gathered up the cones from the practice field. The sun had started setting a little later. Spring was his favorite time of year with the grass freshly cut, the air full of promise and the game fast and furious.

A satisfied feeling flowed through him. The boys were getting it. Slowly, but surely. And Lucy...

What was he going to do about her?

He'd had a tough time focusing during today's practice due to how cute she looked in her pink T-shirt and black shorts. Those sexy legs of her seemed to have gotten longer. Her face glowed from running around.

Look, don't touch. Ryland had been reminding himself of that for the past hour. Okay, the last week and a half.

She held the equipment bag while he put the cones inside. Her sweet scent surrounded him. Man, she smelled good. Fresh and fruity. He took another sniff. Smelling wasn't touching.

"The boys had a good practice today," she said.

"We'll see how they put it to use in their first match."

"Connor said they've never beaten the Strikers." She tightened the pull string on the bag. "Will they be ready?"

"No, but soccer at this age is all about development."

"Scores aren't reported."

He was used to being surrounded by attractive women, but with Lucy her looks weren't her only appeal. He appreciated how she threw herself into learning about soccer, practicing the drills and studying the rules at home. "Maybe not, but the boys will know the score. And I'd be willing to bet so will the majority of the parents."

"Probably," she said, sounding rueful.

Empathy tugged at him. "You might have to deal with that. Especially toward the end of the season."

She nodded, resigned. "I can handle it."

Pride for her "can do" attitude swelled in his chest. "I know you can."

Lucy's unwavering smile during practices suggested she might be falling in love with the game. Too bad she couldn't fall for him, too.

But that wasn't going to happen. She didn't look at him as anything other than her helper.

Many women wanted to go out with a professional athlete. Lucy wasn't impressed by what he did. He could pump gas at the corner filling station for all she cared. She never asked him anything about his "job" only how his foot was doing. Her indifference to him bristled, even if he knew it was less complicated that way.

She scanned the field. "Looks like we've got everything."

Without waiting for a reply, she headed toward the parking lot. He hobbled along behind her, watching her backside and biting his lip to keep from commenting on how sexy she looked in her gym shorts.

Flirting with her came so naturally, he'd tried hard during practices to keep the conversation focused on soccer. Maybe he should try to be more personable. She was back in town, just like him. She could be...lonely.

Ryland fell into step next to Lucy. Maybe he was the one who was lonely. He'd had offers for company from one of the soccer moms and from several other women in town. None had interested him enough to say yes, but something about Lucy...

He knew all the reasons to keep away from her, but he

couldn't stop thinking about her or wanting to spend time with her outside of practice.

Lines creased her forehead, the way they did when she was nervous or worried. "Uh-oh. Look how many parents stayed to watch practice today."

He'd been too busy with the boys and sneaking peeks at Lucy to notice the row of chairs along the edge of the grass. The different colors reminded him of a rainbow. Several dads sat alongside the moms who had come to the last two practices. Some of the men were the same ones who had either ignored or bullied him in elementary school. It wasn't until he'd proven his worth on the pitch that he'd become a real person in their eyes. Now they clamored to talk to him about their sons. "I thought they were too busy or working to be at practices."

"That's what they said when I asked if one of them could coach."

"At least no one can use that excuse now."

Her eyes widened. "You're leaving already?"

Interesting. Lucy sounded upset. Maybe she wasn't as indifferent to him as she appeared to be. "Not yet. But when I do you'll need a new assistant. Maybe two."

"Oh, okay," she said. "It's just the boys like having you around, especially Connor."

"What about you?"

She flinched. "Me?"

Ryland had put her on the spot. He didn't care. The way she reacted to his leaving suggested this wasn't only about the team. If that were true, he wanted to know even if it wouldn't change anything between them. Or change it that much. "Yes, you."

"You're an excellent coach. I'm learning a lot."

"And…"

"A nice guy."

"And…

The color on her cheeks deepened. "A great soccer player."

"Yes, but you haven't seen me play."

"Modest, huh?"

He shrugged.

"Aaron and Connor told me how good you are."

Ryland wouldn't mind showing her just how good he was at a lot more than soccer.

Bad idea. Except...

He knew women. Lucy was more interested in him than she was letting on. His instincts couldn't be that off. Not with her. "You haven't answered my question."

She looked at the grass. "I appreciate you being here."

"Do you like having me around?"

"It doesn't suck," Lucy said finally.

Not a yes, but close enough. The ball had been passed to him. Time to take the shot.

"Bring Connor over tonight. He can walk Cupcake." Ryland might want to be alone with Lucy, but he knew that wasn't going to happen. A nine-year-old chaperone was a good idea, anyway. The last thing this could turn into was a date. "I'll have pizza delivered."

Her jaw tightened. "You don't have to do this."

"Do what?"

"Repay me for dinner."

"I'm not."

"So this is..."

"For Connor." That was all it could be. *For now,* a little voice whispered.

A beat passed. And another. "He'd like that."

Ryland would have preferred hearing she would like that, too. "I'll order pizza, salad and breadsticks."

"I'll bring dessert."

If he told her not to bother, she'd bring something anyway. And this wasn't a date. "Sounds great."

"Ice-cream sundaes, okay?"

"Perfect."

He could think of lots of ways to use the extra whipped cream with Lucy. The cherries, too. Ryland grinned.

But not tonight. He pressed his lips together. Maybe not any night. And that, he realized, was a total bummer.

The Jameses' kitchen was four times the size of Aaron and Dana's and more "gourmet" with granite countertops, stainless-steel top-of-the-line appliances and hi-tech lighting. The luxurious setting seemed a stark contrast to the casual menu. But no one seemed to notice that except Lucy.

She felt as if she were standing on hot coals and hadn't been able to relax all evening. The same couldn't be said about Connor. A wide grin had been lighting her nephew's face since they'd left practice. He seemed completely at home, hanging on Ryland's every word and playing with Cupcake.

That pleased her since she'd accepted Ryland's invitation for Connor's sake. And *Starry Night* hadn't been painted from within the confines of an asylum, either.

Lucy grimaced. Okay, a part of her had wanted to come over, too.

Insane.

She had to be crazy to torture herself by agreeing to spend more time with Ryland outside of practice. Hanging out with him was working about as well as it had when she'd been in middle school. Her insides quivered, making her feel all jittery. She rinsed a dinner plate, needing the mundane task to steady her nerves.

It didn't help much.

Ryland entered the kitchen. The large space seemed smaller, more…intimate.

She squared her shoulders, not about to let him get to her.

"Connor is chasing Cupcake around the backyard," Ryland said. "It's lighted and fenced so you won't have to worry about him."

She loaded the plate into the dishwasher. As long as the conversation remained on Connor she should be fine. "What makes you think I worry?"

"Nothing, except you pay closer attention to your nephew than an armored car guard does to his cargo."

Lucy rinsed another plate. "I'm supposed to watch him."

"I'm kidding." Ryland placed the box with the leftover pizza slices into the refrigerator. "Aaron has nothing to worry about with you in charge."

She thought about her brother and sister-in-law so far away. "I hope you're right. Sometimes…"

"Sometimes?" he asked.

Lucy stared into the sink, wishing she hadn't said anything. Letting her guard down was too easy when Ryland was around. Strange since that was exactly the time she should keep it up.

"Tell me," he said.

Warm water ran over her hands, but did nothing to soothe her. "Until Aaron and Dana deployed, I had no idea what having someone totally rely on you meant. It's not as easy as I thought it would be. Sometimes I don't think I'm as focused on Connor as I should be."

Especially the past week and a half with Ryland on her mind so much.

"Any more focused and you'd be obsessing." He smiled. "Don't worry. Connor is happy. All smiles."

She placed the plate in the dishwasher. "That's because of you."

"Yeah, you're right about that."

Ryland's lighthearted tone told her that he was joking. She turned and flicked her hands at him. Droplets of water flew in his direction.

He jumped back. Amusement filled his gaze.

"Gee, thanks," she joked.

"Seriously, you're doing a great job," Ryland said. "Your kids will be the envy of all their friends."

Her kids? Heat exploded through Lucy like the grand finale of Fourth of July fireworks. Jeff had said she was too independent to be a decent wife. He'd told her that she would be a bad mother. Funny, how his liking a self-reliant girlfriend when they were dating turned out to be one-hundred-and-eighty percent different from his wanting a needy wife to stroke his fragile ego after they married.

"Thanks." She placed a plate in the rack next to the other. "I suppose being a surrogate parent now will help if I ever have a family of my own."

"If?"

She shrugged. "I've got too much going on with Connor to think about the future."

"Nothing wrong with focusing on the present," he said.

Yeah, she imagined that was what he did. But his situation was different from hers. He was doing something with his life. And she...

Lucy picked up the last plate and scrubbed. Hard.

A longing ached deep inside her. She wanted to do something, too. Be someone. To matter...

Uh-oh. She didn't want to end up throwing herself a pity-party. Not with Ryland here. Time to get things back on track.

She loaded the plate. "Connor has been writing his parents about soccer practices and telling them how well you coach."

"I bet Aaron sees right through that."

"Probably."

Ryland raised a brow. "Probably?"

"You said it," she teased.

He picked up the can of whipped cream with one hand and the red cap with his other. "You didn't have to agree."

"Well, Connor did say you're *almost* as good a coach as his dad."

"Almost, huh?" With a grin, Ryland walked toward her. "I thought we were on the same team, but since we're not..."

He pointed the can of whipped cream in her direction.

She stepped back. Her backside bumped into the granite counter. The lowered dishwasher door had her boxed in on the left. Ryland blocked the way on the right. Trapped. It didn't bother her as much as it should. "You wouldn't."

Challenge gleamed in his eyes. "Whipped cream would go well with your outfit."

His, too. They could have so much fun with the whipped cream. Anticipation made her smile.

What was she thinking? Forget about the whipped cream. Forget about him.

Self-preservation made her reach behind and pull the hand nozzle from the sink. She aimed it at him. The surprise in his eyes made her feel strong and competent. Her confidence surged. "I wonder how you'll look all wet."

A corner of his mouth curved and something shifted between them. The air crackled with tension, with heat. His gaze smoldered.

Heaven help her. She swallowed. Thank goodness for the counter's support or she'd be a puddle on the floor.

"I'm game if you are," he said.

For the first time in a long time, Lucy was tempted to...play. But nerves threatened to get the best of her. She knew better to play with fire.

Unsure of what to do or say next, she clutched the nozzle as if it could save her. From what, she wasn't sure.

Still Lucy wasn't ready to back down. Surrendering wasn't an option, either. "What if I'm out of practice and don't remember how to play?"

He took a step toward her. "I'm an excellent coach. I can show you."

She bet he could. She could imagine all kinds of things he could show her. Her cheeks burned. "What are the rules?"

He grinned wryly. "Play fair. Don't cheat."

A little pang hit her heart. "Those sound like good rules. I don't like cheaters."

"Neither do I."

His gaze captured hers. She didn't know how long they stood there with their weapons ready. It didn't matter. Nothing did except this moment with him.

Lucy wanted...a kiss. The realization ricocheted through her, a mix of shock and anticipation. No wonder she held a water nozzle in her hand ready to squirt him. She wanted Ryland to kiss her senseless. If only...

Not possible. She didn't want to get burned. Again.

Still her lips parted slightly. An invitation or a plea of desperation, she wasn't certain.

Desire flared in his eyes.

Please.

She wasn't brave enough to say the word aloud.

"How do I know this isn't a trap?" he asked with mock seriousness.

"I could say the same thing."

"We could put our weapons down on three."

"Fair play."

He stood right in front of her. "Exactly."

She nodded, still gripping the nozzle. "One, two…"

Ryland lowered his mouth to hers. The touch of his lips sent a shock through her. He tasted warm with a hint of chocolate from the hot-fudge topping.

His tender kiss caressed. She felt cherished and important. Ways she hadn't felt in years. Her toes curled. She gripped the nozzle.

This was what had been missing, what she needed.

Bells rang. Mozart. Boy, could Ryland kiss.

She wanted more. Oh-so-much-more.

A dog barked.

Lucy leaned into Ryland, into his kiss. She brought her right arm around him and her left…

Water squirted everywhere.

Ryland jumped back, his shirt wet.

She glanced down. Hers hadn't fared much better. Thank goodness she was wearing a camisole underneath her T-shirt.

Laughter lit his eyes. "At least you got the playing fair part. We're both wet."

Lucy attempted to laugh. She couldn't. She tried to speak. She couldn't do that, either. Not after being so expertly and thoroughly kissed. Ryland's kiss had left her confused, wanting more and on fire despite the water socking her shirt and dripping down her legs.

A crush was one thing. This felt like…

No, it was nothing but some hot kisses.

Lucy straightened. Letting him kiss her had been a momentary lapse in judgment. She should have ended the kiss as soon as his mouth touched hers. But she hadn't. She...couldn't. Worse, her lips wanted more kisses.

Stupid. The word needed to be tattooed across her forehead for the world to see. Correction, for her to see, a reminder of the mistakes she'd made when it came to men.

"Aunt Lucy." Connor ran into the kitchen with Cupcake at his heels. Her nephew stared at her and Ryland with wide eyes. "What happened?"

"An accident," Ryland answered.

Did he mean the kiss or the water? The question hammered at her. She wasn't sure she wanted to know the answer, either.

A sudden realization sent a shiver down Lucy's spine. For the few minutes she'd been kissing Ryland, she hadn't thought once about Connor. He'd been left unattended in a strange house. Okay, Cupcake had been with him and Lucy had only been in the kitchen, but still...

Ryland's kiss had made her forget everything, including her nephew. That could not happen again. She adjusted the hem of her shirt, smoothed her hair and looked at her nephew. "You okay?"

Connor nodded. "But there's a man at the front door. He said his name is Blake. He's here to see Ryland."

CHAPTER SEVEN

STANDING in his parents' living room, Ryland dragged his hand through his hair. Uncomfortable didn't begin to describe the atmosphere. Blake's nostrils flared. A thoroughly kissed and embarrassed Lucy stared at Connor, who sat on the carpet playing with Cupcake, oblivious to what was going on.

Not that any of the adults had a clue.

At least Ryland didn't.

He was trying to figure out what had happened in the kitchen. He couldn't stop thinking about Lucy's kisses. About how silver sparks had flashed when she'd opened her eyes. About how right she felt in his arms.

Not good since the last thing he needed was a woman in his life. Even one as sweet and delicious as Lucy Martin. But this wasn't the time to think about anything except damage control.

Blake hadn't seen them kissing, but Lucy's presence was going to be a problem. A big one.

"Let me introduce everyone," Ryland said.

Polite words were exchanged. Obligatory handshakes given.

Thick tension hung on the air, totally different from the sizzling heat in the kitchen a few minutes ago. That was where Ryland wished he could be now—in the kitchen kissing Lucy.

Whoa. He must have taken a header with a ball too hard and not remembered. Ryland was in enough trouble with his agent. He needed to stop thinking about kisses. And her. Not even flings were in his playbook at the moment.

"What brings you to Wicksburg?" Lucy asked Blake.

Ryland wanted to know the answer to that question, too. Blake never dropped by unannounced. Something big must have happened with either Fuego or his sponsors.

Good news, Ryland hoped. But given the muscle flicking on Blake's jaw and the tense lines around his mouth, probably not.

"I was in Chicago for a meeting." That explained Blake's designer suit, silk tie and Italian-leather shoes. Not exactly comfortable traveling attire, but Blake always dressed well, even when he was straight out of law school and joining the ranks of sports agents. "I thought I'd swing by Indiana and see how Ryland was doing on his own."

Swing by? Yeah, right. No one swung by Wicksburg when the nearest airport was a two-hour drive away. Blake must have rented a car to get here. Something was up. The question was what.

The edges of Lucy's mouth curved upward in a forced smile. The pink flush that had crept up her neck after he'd kissed her hadn't disappeared yet. "That's nice of you."

Blake Cochrane and the word "nice" didn't belong in the same sentence. Of course Lucy wouldn't know that. He had the reputation of being a shark when it came to contract negotiations and pretty much anything else. His hard-nosed toughness made him a great agent. Blake eyed Lucy with suspicion. "I can see my concerns about Ryland being lonely are unfounded."

The agent's ice-blue eyes narrowed to slits. He focused first on Lucy then moved to Ryland.

The accusation in Blake's voice and gaze left no doubt what the agent thought was going on here. Ryland grimaced. He didn't like Lucy being lumped in with other women he'd gone out with. He squared his shoulders. "I invited Lucy and Connor over to take Cupcake on a walk for me and have some pizza."

"And ice-cream sundaes," Connor added with a grin.

Blake's brow slanted. His gaze lingered on Lucy's damp shirt that clung to her breasts like a second skin. "A water fight, too, I see."

Ryland tried hard not to look at her chest. Tried and failed.

The color on Lucy's face deepened. She looked like she wanted to bolt.

His jaw tensed. He didn't like seeing her so uncomfortable. "Faucet malfunction."

"Hate when that happens," Blake said.

Damn him. Blake wasn't happy finding Lucy here, but he didn't have to be such a jerk about it. Ryland's hands balled. "Nothing that can't be fixed."

His harsh tone silenced the living room. Only Connor and the dog seemed at ease.

"Well, it's been nice meeting you, Blake. It's a school night so we have to get home," Lucy said. "Thanks for having us over for dinner, Ryland."

"Yeah, thanks. I had fun with Cupcake." Connor stood, stifling a yawn. "This is a cool house. The backyard is so big we could hold our practices here."

"You play soccer?" Blake asked.

Connor nodded.

Blake studied the kid, as if sizing up his potential. Scouts could recognize talent at a young age. In the United Kingdom, the top prospects signed with football clubs in their teens. "What position do you play?"

Connor raised his chin, a gesture both his dad and Lucy made. "Wherever I'm told to play."

Blake's sudden smile softened his rugged features. "With that kind of attitude you'll go far."

Connor beamed. "I want to be just like Ryland when I grow up."

The words touched him. He mussed Connor's hair. Working with the boys reminded him of the early years of playing soccer, full of fun, friendship and laughter. "Thanks, bud."

Ryland turned his attention to Lucy. He wanted to kiss her good-night. Who was he kidding? He wanted to kiss her hello, goodbye and everything in between. She was sexy and sweet, a potent, addictive combo. He should have his head examined soon. There wasn't room in his life for a serious girlfriend, especially one who lived in Wicksburg. He couldn't afford to lose his edge now. "I'll see you out."

Lucy nodded.

That surprised him. He'd expected her to say it wasn't necessary like the first time she'd visited.

"I'll stay here," Blake said.

Ryland accompanied them to the driveway where Lucy's car was parked. Lights on either side of the garage door illuminated the area. Cupcake ran around the car barking. She didn't seem to want Connor to go. Ryland felt the same way about Lucy.

That made zero sense. They weren't playing house. Being with her wasn't cozy. More like being on a bed of hot knives. She needed to leave before he got the urge to kiss her again.

Connor climbed into the backseat. Cupcake followed, but Ryland lifted the dog out of the car and held on to her. As soon as Connor fastened his seat belt, his eyelids closed.

"He's out," Ryland said.

She glanced back at the house. "You're in trouble."

The word "no" sat on the tip of his tongue and stayed there. He didn't want to worry Lucy, but he also didn't want to lie. Blake's surprise visit concerned Ryland. "I don't know."

Lines creased Lucy's forehead. Her gaze, full of concern and compassion, met his. "Blake doesn't look happy."

Ryland was a lone wolf kind of guy. He wasn't used to people being concerned about him. It made him…uncomfortable.

Best not to think about that. Or her. "Blake's intense. No one would ever accuse him of being mild-mannered and laid-back."

"I wouldn't want to meet him in a dark alley. A good thing he's on your side."

"Blake's my biggest supporter after my folks." The agent had always been there for Ryland. One of the few people who had believed in him from the beginning. "He fights for his clients. I've been with him for eleven years. I was the second client to sign with him."

"You both must have been young then."

"Young and idealistic." Those had been the days before all

the other stuff—the business stuff—became such a priority and a drag. "But we've grown up and been through a lot."

"You've probably made him a bunch of money over the years."

They were both rich men now. "Yeah."

But her words made Ryland think. Those closest to him, besides his parents, were people who made money off him. His agent, his PR spokesperson, his trainer, the list went on. His friends were plentiful when he was covering the tab at a club or throwing a party, but not so much now that he was stuck in the middle-of-nowhere Indiana. Bitterness coated his mouth.

Was that the reason Blake had dropped by? To make sure his income from "Ryland James" endorsements and licensing agreements wouldn't dry up?

Ryland hoped not. He wanted to think he was considered more than just a client after all the years.

The tip of her pink tongue darted out to moisten her lips.

He wouldn't mind another taste of her lips. He fought the urge to pull her against him and kiss her until the worry disappeared. "About what happened in the kitchen…"

The lines on her forehead deepened. She glanced at Connor who was asleep. "That shouldn't have happened. It was a… mistake."

Ryland studied her, trying to figure out what she was thinking. He couldn't. "It didn't feel like a mistake."

"I…"

He placed his finger against her lips, remembering how soft they'd felt against his own. They needed to talk, but this wasn't the time, and maybe the words needed to remain unsaid. "It's late."

"Blake's waiting for you."

"Don't let the suit and attitude fool you. He's not in charge here. I am," Ryland said. "Take Connor home. We'll talk soon."

She nodded.

"Blake's bag was in the entryway. He's staying the night."

An ache formed deep in Ryland's gut. He wanted to kiss Lucy. More than he'd wanted anything in a long time. He didn't understand why he was feeling that way. Staying away from her was the smart thing to do. Though come to think of it, no one had ever accused him of being smart. "I'll call you tomorrow. Promise."

So much for playing it safe. But something about Lucy made him forget reason and make promises.

She started to speak then stopped herself. "Good luck with Blake."

"Thanks, but I've got all the luck I need thanks to your penny."

Her eyes widened. "You kept it?"

Bet she'd be surprised to know the penny had been sitting on his nightstand for the past two weeks. "Never know when I'll need it to get lucky."

The color on her cheeks deepened again. "That's my cue to say good-night."

Sweet and smart. It was a good thing Blake was going to be his houseguest tonight and not Lucy. Ryland opened the car door for her. "Drive safe."

After the taillights of Lucy's car faded from view, he went inside. He couldn't put off his conversation with Blake any longer.

His agent stood in the entryway. He'd changed into shorts, a T-shirt and running shoes.

"Tell me what you're really doing here," Ryland said.

"I've been on airplanes or stuck at conference tables for the last two days," Blake said. "Let's work out."

In the home gym, Ryland hopped on the stationary bike. His physical therapist had increased the number of things he could do as his foot healed. He liked being able to do more exercises, but working out was the furthest thing from his mind. Thoughts about Lucy and her hot kisses as well as his agent's purpose for coming here filled his brain.

Blake stepped on the treadmill. He adjusted the settings on the computerized control panel. "I knew you couldn't go that long without a woman."

Ryland's temper flared. But after receiving more red cards

these past two seasons than all the seasons before, he'd learned not to react immediately. He accelerated his pedaling, instead. "You're checking up on me."

"Sponsors are nervous." Blake's fast pace didn't affect his speech or breathing. "They aren't the only ones."

So now his agent had added babysitter to his list of duties. Great. Ryland's fingers tightened around the handlebars. "You."

"I don't get nervous." Blake accelerated his pace. "But I am...concerned. You'll be thirty soon. We need to make the most of the next few years whether you're playing with Fuego or across the pond."

His agent had stressed the need for financial planning to Ryland since he was eighteen years old. But he'd never set out to amass a fortune, just be the best soccer player he could be. "I'm set for life."

"You can never have too much money when you're earning potential will drastically diminish once you stop playing."

Ryland had more money than he could ever spend, but dissatisfaction gnawed at him. He might be injured, but he wasn't about to be put out to pasture just yet.

"Don't be concerned. I'm laying low," he said. "Tonight is the first time I've had anyone over to the house other than the housekeeper, who's old enough to be my mom. I made sure Lucy and I had a chaperone."

"Nice kid," Blake said. "Is it his team you're coaching?"

Damn. Ryland slowed his pedaling. He reached for his water bottle off the nearby counter then took a long swig. The cool liquid rushing down his throat did little to refresh him. "Where'd you hear that?"

"Someone tweeted you were coaching a local rec. team." Blake kept a steady pace. "Tell me this was some sort of one-off rah-rah-isn't-soccer-great pep talk."

"I'm helping Lucy with Connor's team." Ryland placed his water bottle on the counter. "Her brother coaches the team, but he's on deployment with his Reserve unit. No other parent stepped up so she took on the role as head coach even though she knows nothing about soccer. I offered to help."

"Lucy's so hot she could get a man to do most anything," Blake said. "Those legs of hers go on forever."

The appreciative gleam in his agent's ice-blue eyes bugged Ryland. Women always swarmed around Blake. He didn't need to be checking out Lucy, too.

Ryland's jaw tensed. "I'm coaching for both her and the boys."

"Mostly Lucy, though." Blake grinned. "That's a good thing."

"It is?"

"Your coaching becomes a nonissue if you have a personal connection and aren't showing favoritism to one team."

"Favoritism?" Ryland didn't understand what Lucy had to do with this. "I'm helping the Defeeters, but I've also spoken to two other teams this week and will visit with three more next week."

"No need to get defensive," Blake said. "A guy helping out his girlfriend isn't showing favoritism."

Girlfriend? A knot formed in the pit of Ryland's stomach. Everything suddenly made sense. "So if Lucy and I aren't..."

He couldn't bring himself to say the word.

Blake nodded. "If you weren't dating Lucy, you wouldn't be able to coach the team."

Ryland's knuckles turned white. "What do you mean?"

As Blake moved from the treadmill to the stair-climber machine, he wiped the sweat from his face with a white towel. "You're public property. The face of the Phoenix Fuego. Showing favoritism to one team without a valid personal connection would be a big no-no for a player of your caliber. Especially one on shaky ground already."

Ryland gulped.

"But we don't need to worry about that," Blake added.

Emotion tightened Ryland's throat. His agent had always been overprotective. No doubt watching over his investment. Ryland understood that, but he wasn't going back on his word to help Lucy with the team. She needed him. "No worries."

If his agent believed a romance was going on between

Ryland and Lucy, Blake wouldn't feel the need to play mother hen. No one would have to know the truth. Not the sponsors or the Fuego, not even Lucy...

Play fair. Don't cheat.

Not saying anything wasn't cheating, but it wasn't exactly fair, either.

"I must admit I'm a little surprised," Blake said. "Lucy's not your usual type."

Ryland wasn't sure he had a type, but the kind of women he met at clubs couldn't hold a candle to a certain fresh-faced woman with a warm smile, big heart and legs to her neck. Someone who didn't care how much he made or the club he played for or what car he drove. Someone whose kisses had rocked his world.

"I've known Lucy since she was in kindergarten," Ryland explained. "Her brother was one of my closest friends and teammates when I was growing up."

Blake's brows furrowed. "We might be able to use this to our advantage. McElroy is big on family. Childhood sweethearts reunited would make a catchy headline."

Whoa, so not going there. "Lucy was too young for me to date when we were in school. Don't try to milk this for something it's not. I'll be leaving town soon."

"The two of you seem cozy. Serious."

Ryland climbed off the bike. "I don't do serious."

"You haven't done serious. That doesn't mean you can't," Blake said. "Lucy could be a keeper."

Definitely.

The renegade thought stopped Ryland cold. Lucy might be a keeper, but not for him. Fame and adoring women hadn't always satisfied him, but things would improve now that he'd had a break. This time away was what he needed. He could concentrate on his career and get back on track with the same hunger and edge that had made him a star player.

Besides Lucy needed a guy who would be around to help her with Connor. Someone who could make her a priority and give her the attention she deserved. He couldn't be that kind of guy, not when he played soccer all over the world, lived in Arizona and wasn't about to start thinking in the long-term until his career was over.

Ryland picked up his water bottle. "The only keeper I want in my life is a goalkeeper."

There wasn't room for any other kind. There just couldn't be.

While a tired Connor brushed his teeth, Lucy laid out his pajamas on his bed. She couldn't stop thinking about Ryland. About his kissing her. About what he might be saying to his agent right now.

Lucy wished she could turn back the clock. She would have turned down his offer to come over tonight. That way he wouldn't be in trouble and she wouldn't want more of his kisses.

Pathetic.

Crushing on Ryland didn't mean she should be kissing him. Crushes were supposed to be fun, not leave her with swollen lips and a confused heart.

Not her heart, she corrected herself. Her mind.

Her heart was fine. Safe. She planned on keeping it that way. Keeping her distance from Ryland would be her best plan of action. She wasn't supposed to see him again until the Defeeters' game on Saturday. Though he'd promised he would call tomorrow...

He'd used the word "promise" again. He hadn't let her down the first time. She hoped he wouldn't this time, but she had no idea. She didn't trust herself when it came to men.

Lucy's fingers twitched. Touching her tingling lips for the umpteenth time would not help matters. She needed to hold a pencil and sketchbook. She needed to draw.

As soon as Connor was in bed...

He was her priority. Not her art. Definitely not Ryland.

The phone rang.

Her heart leaped. Ryland. Oh, boy, she had it bad.

Connor darted out of the bathroom as if he'd gotten his second wind. He picked up the telephone receiver. "Hello, this is Connor, may I ask who's calling…Dad!"

The excitement in that one word brought a big smile to Lucy's face. Relief, too. Aaron must have returned to a base where phone calls could be made. Her brother was safe. For now.

"I'm so glad you got my emails." Connor leaned against the wall. "Yeah. Ryland knows a lot about soccer. He's cool. But no one is as good a coach as you…We had dinner at his house tonight…Pizza…No, just me and Aunt Lucy. I got to walk his parents' dog. Her name is Cupcake…Can we get a dog?…Ryland said they were a lot of work…" Connor nodded at whatever Aaron said to him. "Yeah, he's a nice guy just like you said…Okay…I love you, too." Connor handed Lucy the phone. "Dad wants to talk to you."

That was odd. Usually she emailed Aaron and Dana so they could spend their precious phone minutes speaking with Connor. She raised the phone to her ear. "Hey, Bro. Miss you."

"Ryland James?" Aaron asked.

Her brother's severe tone made her shoo Connor into his bedroom. "Ryland's helping with Connor's team."

"Dinner at his house has nothing to do with the *team*."

She walked down the hallway to put some distance between her and her nephew. "Connor likes spending time with him."

"And you're hanging with Ryland for the sake of Connor?"

"Yes. Connor's the reason I accepted the dinner invitation." She kept her voice low so her nephew wouldn't hear. "He misses you and Dana so much. But ever since Ryland started working with the team, Connor's been happy and all smiles."

"What about you?" Aaron asked. "You had a big crush on him."

"That was years ago," she said.

"Ryland James is a player, Luce. You don't follow soccer, but I do. The guy has a bad reputation when it comes to women. He'll break your heart if he gets the chance."

"I'll admit he's attractive," she said. "But after Jeff, I know better than to fall for a guy like Ryland James."

"I hope so."

Her brother sounded doubtful. "Don't worry. Ryland isn't going to be around much longer."

"Stay away from him."

"Hard to do when he's helping me with the team and teaching me what I need to coach."

"Limit your interaction to soccer. I hate to think he might hurt you," Aaron said. "Damn. Out of time. Love you. Be careful, Luce."

The line disconnected.

A lump of emotion formed in her throat. Aaron had tried to warn her about Jeff before she eloped, but Lucy hadn't listened. She couldn't make the same mistake again. Because she knew Aaron was right. Ryland James was dangerous. He could break her heart. Easily. She'd survived when that happened with Jeff. She wasn't sure she could survive that type of heartache again.

Lucy put away the phone receiver and made her way to Connor's bedroom. Aaron's words echoed through her head. She felt like an idiot. She'd questioned whether she could trust Ryland, yet she'd kissed him tonight and still wanted more kisses.

So not good.

But she couldn't wallow or overanalyze. She'd done enough of that when her marriage had ended. She knew what to do now—start a new project. As soon as her nephew was tucked into bed, she would gather her art supplies.

Forget a pencil and sketchbook. Time to pull out the big guns—brushes, paints and canvas. Painting was the only thing that might clear her thoughts enough so she could forget about Ryland James and his kisses.

CHAPTER EIGHT

AFTER Connor left for school the next morning, Lucy worked. She enjoyed graphic design—creative, yet practical—but the painting she'd started last night called to her in a way her normal work never had. She emailed a proof to one client and uploaded changes to another's website. The rest of the items on her To Do list could wait until later.

Lucy stood in front of the painting. The strong, bright, vivid colors filled the canvas. The boldness surprised her.

She wasn't that into abstract art. She preferred subjects that captured a snapshot of life or told a story. But thanks to Ryland, her thoughts and emotions were a mismatched jumble. Geometric shapes, lines and arcs were about all she could manage at the moment.

Still the elements somehow worked. Not too surprising, Lucy supposed. She'd always found solace in art, when she was sick and after her marriage ended. The only difference was this time neither her health nor heart were involved.

She wouldn't allow her heart to be involved. That internal organ would only lead her astray.

Stop thinking. Just paint.

Time to lose herself in the work. Lucy dipped her brush into the paint.

She worked with almost a manic fervor. Joy and sorrow, desire and heartache appeared beneath her brush in bold strokes, bright colors, swirls and slashes.

The doorbell rang.

The sound startled her. She dripped paint onto her hand.

A quick glance at the clock showed she'd been painting for the past two hours. She'd lost track of time. A good thing she'd been interrupted or she could have stayed here all day.

Using a nearby rag, she wiped her hands then headed to the front door. Most likely the UPS man. She'd ordered some paper samples for a client.

Lucy opened the door.

Ryland stood on the porch. Her breath caught and held in her chest. He wore warm-up pants and a matching jacket with a white T-shirt underneath. The casual attire looked stylish on him. His hair was styled, but he hadn't shaved the stubble from his face this morning. Dark circles ringed his eyes, as if he hadn't slept much last night.

Like her.

Though she doubted she'd played a role in his dreams the way he'd starred in hers.

He smiled. "Good morning."

Ryland was the last person she expected to see. He'd told her he would call, not show up in person. But a part of her was happy to see him standing here.

That bothered her. She blew out a breath. Remember what Aaron had said. Ryland was the last person she should want to spend any time with. Yet...

Her gaze slid from his hazel-green eyes to his mouth. Tingles filled her stomach. Her lips ached for another kiss.

Lucy clutched the doorknob. For support or ease in slamming shut the door, she wasn't certain. "What are you doing here?"

Her tone wasn't polite. She didn't care. His presence disturbed her.

His smile faltered a moment before widening. "Let's go for coffee."

"I'm not sure that's such a good idea."

Talk about a wimpy response. She knew going out would be a very bad idea.

"We need to talk about my coaching the Defeeters," he added.

He would bring up coaching and the Defeeters. She was torn. Seeing him over something soccer-related didn't make Ryland James any less dangerous. She glanced down at her paint-splattered shirt and sweatpants. "I'm not dressed to go out."

His gaze took in her clothes and her hands with splotches of purple on them. "You've been painting."

She didn't understand why he sounded so pleased. "Yes."

"We can stay here," he said. "I'd like to see what you're working on."

Lucy didn't feel comfortable sharing her work with Ryland. No way did she want to expose such an intimate part of herself. Not after kissing him had brought up all these feelings. Speaking of kissing him, being alone in the house wasn't a good idea at all. "We can go to the coffee shop. Let me wash up and get my purse."

A few minutes later, refreshed and ready, she locked the front door. "Do you want to meet there?"

"We can ride together."

That was what she was afraid he would say. "I'll drive."

"Your car is nicer than my dad's old truck."

"My car is closer." She motioned to her car parked on the driveway. "Less walking for you."

He headed to her car. "That's thoughtful."

More like self-preservation. She would also be in control. She could determine when they left, not him.

Lucy unlocked the car and opened the door for him. "Do you need help getting in?"

He drew his brows together. "Thanks, but I can handle it."

She walked around the front of the car, slid into her seat and turned on the engine. "Buckled in?"

Ryland patted the seat belt. "All set."

The tension in the air matched her tight jaw. She backed out of the driveway. "So what did you want to talk about?"

"Let's wait until we get to the coffee shop," Ryland said.

They were only five minutes away. She turned on the radio. A pop song with lyrics about going home played. The music was better than silence, but not by much. She tapped her thumbs on the steering wheel. "Does it have anything to do with Blake?"

Ryland nodded. "But no need to worry."

Easier said then done.

Lucy turned onto Main Street. Small shops and restaurants lined the almost-empty street. A quiet morning in Wicksburg. She parked on the street right in front of the Java Bean, a narrow coffee shop with three tables inside and two out front on the sidewalk.

A bell jangled when Ryland opened the door for her. She stepped inside. The place was empty. As they walked to the counter, he placed his hand at the small of her back. His gentle touch made her wish she were back in his arms again, even if that was the last place she should be.

Lucy ordered a cappuccino. He got a double espresso. She went to remove her wallet, but he was handing the barista a twenty-dollar bill.

"You can buy the next time," he said.

Going out to coffee with Ryland was not something she planned on doing again. She'd figure out another way to repay him.

Once their order was ready, she sat at a small, round table. Jazzy instrumental music played from hidden speakers.

Ryland sat across from her. His left foot brushed hers. "Excuse me."

"Sorry." Lucy placed her feet under her chair. The sooner they got this over with the better. She wrapped her hands around the warm mug. "So what's going on?"

Ryland took a sip of his coffee. "Somebody tweeted I was coaching a team of kids in Wicksburg."

"Blake saw the tweet?"

"A PR firm I use did."

She drank from her cup. "No wonder Blake looked so upset."

"He calmed down after you left," Ryland said. "Turns out

helping my girlfriend coach a team is a perfectly acceptable thing for me to do."

Girlfriend? She stared at him confused. "Huh?"

"Blake thinks you and I are dating," Ryland explained.

Dating. The word echoed through her head. Even if the idea appealed to her a tiny, almost miniscule bit, she knew it would never happen. "How did he react when you told him we weren't dating?"

"I didn't tell him." Ryland wouldn't meet her gaze. "I didn't deny we were dating, but I didn't say we were a couple, either."

She stared in disbelief. "So Blake thinks we are—"

"I had no choice."

"There's always a choice." She knew that better than anyone. Sometimes the hard choice was the best option.

"I made my choice."

"You had to do what you thought was best for your career. I get that." He'd gotten into this mess with his agent for helping the Defeeters. She couldn't be angry. "I know how much soccer means to you."

His eyes narrowed. "It's not only about my career. If I'd told Blake we weren't dating, I wouldn't be able to help you and the team."

His words sunk in. Ryland hadn't been thinking of himself. He'd done this for her, Connor and the boys.

Her heart pounded so loudly she was sure the barista behind the counter could hear it.

"I wasn't sure if I should tell you," Ryland admitted.

"Why did you?" she asked.

"Fair play."

Play fair. Don't cheat. She remembered the rules he'd told her last night. Right before he'd kissed her senseless. "Thank you for being honest."

"If it's any consolation, I told Blake we weren't serious about each other."

She was glad they were on the same page about not getting involved except she couldn't ignore a twinge of disappointment.

Silly reaction given the circumstances. "Understatement of the year."

Amusement gleamed in his eyes. "True, but people will believe what they want if we don't deny it. And this way I can keep helping you and the team."

Her heart dropped. "You want us to pretend to be dating."

"It's not what I want, but what we have to do." Ryland's smile reached all the way to his eyes. "After those kisses last night, I'm not sure how much pretending is going to be involved."

Heat flooded her face. "We agreed kissing was a mistake."

"You said that. I didn't." His gaze held hers. "There's chemistry between us."

A highly combustible reaction, but she would never admit it. If she did, Ryland could use it to his advantage. She wouldn't stand a chance if he did.

"This is crazy." Lucy's voice sounded stronger than she felt. She tightened her grip on the coffee-cup handle to keep her hand from shaking. "No more kissing. No pretend dating, either."

"Then you'd better find yourself a new assistant before the game on Saturday."

"Seriously?"

He nodded once.

Darn. Lucy watched steam rise from her coffee cup. She didn't know what to do. She needed to protect herself, but she also had to think about Connor.

Connor.

He was the reason she'd approached Ryland in the first place. Her nephew would be the one to suffer if he couldn't continue coaching the Defeeters. She couldn't allow that to happen.

She tried to push all the other stuff out of her mind, including her own worries, doubts and fears, and to focus on Connor. "What's important here is…the team."

"Especially Connor," Ryland said.

She nodded. What was best for Connor might not be the best thing for her, but so what? She had to put her nephew first even if it put her in an awkward position. "You're leaving soon. Until then I'm willing to do whatever it takes so you can keep coaching the team. I can't imagine it'll be that big a deal to pretend to date since your agent lives in California."

"The other coaches in the rec. league have to believe it, or there could be trouble," Ryland clarified. "The parents, too."

Maybe a bigger deal than she realized. But for her nephew she would do it. "Okay."

"Right now there's no press coverage, but that could change."

This had disaster written all over it. If Aaron found out… She couldn't think about him. Connor was her priority, not her brother.

No matter what life had thrown at Lucy, she'd proven she was capable and able to handle anything. She would do the same here. "It's only for a few weeks, right?"

Ryland nodded. "It'll be fun."

There was that word again. She doubted this would be fun. But as long as he was working with the team, keeping a smile on Connor's face and teaching her how to coach, it would be… doable.

Besides they were just pretending. What could go wrong?

Pretending to date wasn't turning out to be all that great. So far "dating" had amounted to several texts being exchanged about soccer and an impromptu dinner at the pizza parlor with the entire team. He'd have to step things up as soon as this game was over.

It couldn't end quickly enough for Ryland. He forced himself to stay seated on the bench. The Defeeters were outmatched and losing. He couldn't do a single thing about it, either.

"Great job, Defeeters!" Lucy stood along the sideline in a blue T-shirt with the name of the soccer league across the front and warm-up pants. She held a clipboard with a list of when players should be substituted to ensure equal playing time and waved it in the air when she got excited during the game. "You can do it!"

The way she cheered was cute. If only the team could pull

off a victory, but that would take a miracle given their competition today.

Lucy glanced back at him with a big smile on her face. "The boys have improved over the past two weeks."

Ryland nodded. They had lots of work to do at the next practice.

Lucy checked the stopwatch she wore around her neck. "There can't be much time left."

He glanced at his cell phone. "Less than four minutes."

Connor stole the ball from a small, speedy forward. He passed the ball to Marco, who ran toward the field. He dribbled around a defender and another one.

Parents cheered. Lucy waved the clipboard. Ryland shook his head. Marco needed to pass before the ball got stolen.

The kid sped across the center line.

No way could he take the ball all the way to the goal alone. Not against a skilled team like the Strikers.

"Pass," Ryland called out.

Lucy pointed to Jacob, who stood down field with no defenders around him.

"Cross, Marco," Ryland yelled. "To Jacob."

Marco continued dribbling. A tall, blond-haired defender from the opposite team ran up, stole the ball and kicked it to a teammate. Goal.

The Defeeter parents sighed. The Striker parents cheered.

The referee blew the whistle.

Game over. The Defeeters had lost six–three. Not that the league kept score, but still...

Ryland would add some new drills and review the old ones. The boys needed to learn to pass the ball and talk to each other out on the field. This was a soccer match, not Sunday services at church.

Each of the teams shouted cheers. Great. The kids had found their voices now that the game was over.

The players lined up with the coaches at the end and shook hands with their opponents. Several of the Strikers grabbed

their balls and asked Ryland to sign them. He happily obliged
and posed for pictures.

By the time he finished, Lucy was seated on the grass with
the boys. He walked their way, passing through a group of
Defeeter parents.

Suzy, one of the moms, smiled at him. "They played well
out there."

Cheryl nodded. "The last time they played the Strikers it
was a shutout."

Marco's dad, Ewan, patted Ryland on the back. "This is the
most competitive they've ever been. You've done a great job
preparing them."

Interesting. Ryland would have thought the parents would
be upset, but they sounded pleased. The boys were all smiles,
too.

"Did you see?" Connor asked him. "We scored three goals."

Ryland had never seen so many happy faces after a loss.
"Nice match, boys."

"Coach Lucy said if we could score one more goal than the
last time we'd played the Strikers that would be a win in her
book," Marco said.

Dalton pumped his fists in the air. "We needed one goal,
but we scored three!"

Ryland had been so focused on winning he'd forgotten there
was more to a game than the final score. Especially when skills
development, not winning the game, was the goal. But Lucy,
who might not have the technical knowledge, had known that.

She sat with a wide smile on her face and sun-kissed cheeks.
Lovely.

A warm feeling settled over Ryland. They really needed to
spend more time together.

"In the fall, we lost nine–zero," Connor explained.

Ouch. Ryland forced himself not to grimace. No wonder
there was so much excitement over today's match. "You gave
them a much better game today."

Dalton nodded. "We play them again at the end of the season."

"Let's not get ahead of ourselves. This is our first game," Lucy said. "We have lots to work on before that final match."

"I'll second that," Ryland agreed. "But that's what practice is for. All of you played so well today it's time for a celebration."

"Snacks!" the boys yelled in unison.

Suzy, the snack mom for today's game, passed out brown lunch bags filled with juice, string cheese, a package of trail mix and a bag of cookies. The boys attacked the food like piranhas.

Ryland walked over to Lucy, who jotted notes on her clipboard. "Snacks have improved since I played rec. soccer."

"Yes, but the game's still the same."

He didn't want things to stay the same between them.

Sitting behind her, he placed his hands on her shoulders.

Her muscles tensed beneath his palms.

Ryland didn't care. They were supposed to be dating. Might as well start pretending now. Kisses might be off-limits, but she hadn't said anything about not touching. As he placed his mouth by her ear, her sweet scent enveloped him.

"I wanted to congratulate you," he whispered, noticing curious looks from parents and the other coaches. "Excellent job, Coach."

She turned her head toward him. Her lips were mere inches from his. It would be so easy to steal a kiss. But he wasn't going to push it. At least not yet.

Wariness filled her eyes, but she smiled at him. "Thanks, but I have the best assistant coach in the league. The boys wouldn't have scored any goals without his help."

Her warm breath against his skin raised his temperature twenty degrees. He could practically taste her. His mouth watered. Pretend kisses would probably feel just as nice as real ones.

"Though you're going to have to explain the offside rule to me again," she continued. "I still don't get it."

Ryland laughed. Here he was thinking about kisses, and she

was still talking soccer. "I'll keep explaining until you understand it."

Waiting until Monday afternoon to see her again was unacceptable. He doubted she'd agree to a date, not even a pretend one. But she'd agreed to the pretending because of Connor. The kid would give Ryland the perfect reason to see Lucy before the next practice.

Not cheating, he thought. Perhaps not playing one hundred percent fair, but being able to spend some time with her was worth it. Once they were alone, she might even agree.

Ryland stood. "The way you boys played today deserves a special treat." He looked each boy in the eyes. "Who's up for a slushie?"

Sitting on a picnic bench outside Rocket Burgers, Lucy placed her mouth around the straw sticking out of her cup and sipped her blue-raspberry slushie. Suzy, Cheryl, Debbie and the other moms from the team sat with her.

Ryland and the dads sat with the boys on a grassy area near a play structure.

Suzy set her cup on the table. "Ryland is so nice to treat us all to slushies."

"I'm sure he can afford it. You are so lucky Lucy to spend so much time with him." Cheryl pouted. "I thought I had a chance, but it's better he chose you since I'm not divorced."

Suzy smiled at Lucy. "I thought you guys looked a little chummier at the pizza party, but I didn't realize you were dating until today."

"He is a total catch," Debbie said. "The two of you make a cute couple."

Happiness shot all the way to the tips of Lucy's hot-pink painted toenails. Not for her, she countered. But for Connor. This charade was for him. She repositioned her straw. "Thanks."

Lucy was not going to confirm or deny anything about their "dating." The less she said, the less dishonest she would feel. She drank more of her slushie.

The men laughed. The boys, too. Through the cacophony

of noise, the squeals and giggles, Lucy singled out Ryland's laughter. The rich sound curled around her heart and sent her temperature climbing. She sipped her slushie, but the icy drink did nothing to cool her down.

No biggie. She would be heading home soon and wouldn't have to see Ryland until Monday afternoon.

As the women talked about a family who'd moved to Iowa, Lucy glanced his way. Ryland sat with Connor on one side and Dalton on the other, the only two boys on the team without fathers here today.

While the other boys spoke with their fathers, Ryland talked to Connor and Dalton. The boys looked totally engaged in the conversation. Smiles lit up their faces. They laughed.

A soccer ball–size lump formed in her throat.

Ryland James might have a reputation as a womanizer, but she could tell someday he would be a great dad. The kind of dad she had. The kind of dad her brother was.

He flashed her a lopsided grin and winked.

Lucy had been caught staring. She should look away, but she didn't want to. She realized since they were pretending to date she didn't have to.

The fluttery sensations in her stomach reminded her of when she was thirteen and head over heels in love with Ryland. But she knew better than to fantasize about a happily ever after now with a guy like him. Besides she knew happy endings were rare, almost nonexistent these days.

A dad named Chuck said something to Ryland. He looked at him, breaking the connection with her.

Lucy turned her attention to the table. The other women had gotten up except for Suzy.

"Well, this has been fun." Cheryl motioned to her son Dalton and gazed longingly at Ryland. "See you at practice on Monday."

"The boys will have their work cut out for them," he said.

Families said goodbye and headed to their cars. Several boys lagged behind, not wanting to leave their friends. Marco and Connor ran up to the picnic table. Ryland followed them.

"Can Connor spend the night?" Marco asked his mom.

"Sure. We have no plans other than to hang out and watch a DVD." Suzy glanced at Lucy. "Is it okay with you?"

Connor stared at her with an expectant look. "Please, Aunt Lucy?"

"He's had sleepovers at our house before," Suzy added.

Dana had provided Lucy with the names of acceptable sleepover and playdate friends. Marco had been at the top of the list. "Okay."

The boys gave each other high fives.

"But you're going to have to come home with me first. You need to shower and pack your things," she said.

"I have to run by the grocery store. We can pick him up on our way home," Suzy offered.

"Thanks." Lucy hugged her nephew. "This will be my first night alone since I've been back in Wicksburg. I don't know what I'll do."

Connor slipped out of her embrace. "Ryland can keep you company tonight."

She started to speak, but Ryland beat her to it.

"I have no plans tonight," he said. "I'd be happy to make sure your aunt doesn't miss you too much."

The mischievous look on Ryland's face made her wonder if he'd planned this whole thing. She wouldn't put it past him. But a part of her was flattered he'd go to so much trouble to spend time with her.

Remember, it's pretend.

"Then we're all set." Suzy grinned. "See you in an hour or so."

As Marco and his parents headed to their SUV, Connor watched them go. "Tonight is going to be so much fun."

Maybe for him. Anxiety built inside Lucy. She had no idea if Ryland was serious about tonight. A part of her hoped he was serious about keeping her company. Not because she was going to be lonely, but because she wanted to see him.

Ridiculous. She blew out a puff of air.

"I'll see you at five," Ryland said.

Before she could say anything he walked off toward the old beat-up truck.

Okay, he was serious. But what exactly did he have in mind?

Connor bounced on his toes. "We'd better get home."

She wrapped her arm around his thin shoulders. "You have plenty of time to get ready for your sleepover."

"I'm not worried about me, but Dad says it takes Mom hours to get ready. You're going to need a lot of time."

His words and sage tone amused her. "What for?"

"Your date with Ryland."

Lucy flinched. She hadn't wanted to drag Connor into the ruse. "Date?"

"Ryland's taking you out to dinner." A smug smile settled on Connor's freckled face. "I told him Otto's was your favorite restaurant, and you liked the cheese fondue best. I also told him it was expensive and only for special occasions, but Ryland said he could probably afford it."

"He can." He could probably afford to buy the entire town.

"If you and Ryland got married, that would make him my new uncle, right?" Connor asked.

Oh, no. The last thing she needed was Connor mentioning marriage to Aaron. "Marriage is serious business. Ryland and I are just going out to eat."

"But it would be pretty cool, don't ya think?"

Maybe if she were nine she would think it was cool. But she was twenty-six and pretending to be dating a soccer star. Marriage was the last thing on her mind while she took care of Connor for the next year. She wasn't even sure if she wanted to get married again. Not after Jeff.

"When two people love each other, marriage can be very cool," Lucy said carefully. "But love is not something you can rush. It takes time."

"My dad knew the minute he saw my mom he was going to marry her," Connor said. "They didn't date very long."

"That's true, but what happened with your mom and dad doesn't happen to many people."

Definitely not her and Jeff.

"But it could happen with you and Ryland," Connor said optimistically.

She gave him a squeeze. "I suppose anything is possible."

But in her and Ryland's case, highly unlikely.

CHAPTER NINE

STANDING on Lucy's front door step on Saturday night, Ryland held the single iris behind his back. At the flower shop, he'd headed straight for the roses because that was what he usually bought women, but the purple flower caught his eyes. The vibrant color reminded him of Lucy, so full of life. He hoped she liked it.

Anticipation for his "date" buzzed through Ryland. He hadn't gone to this much trouble for a woman before. Not unless you counted what he did for his mom on Mother's Day, her birthday in July and Christmastime. But like his mother, Lucy was worth it. Even if this wasn't a "real" date.

He wanted her to see how much fun they could have together. And it would be a memory he could take with him when he left Wicksburg. One he hoped Lucy would look back on fondly herself. Smiling, he pressed the doorbell.

A moment later, the door opened.

Lucy stood in the doorway. Mascara lengthened her eyelashes. Pink gloss covered her lips. He couldn't tell if she was wearing any other makeup. Not that she needed any with her high cheekbones and wide-set eyes.

She never wore any jewelry other than a watch, but tonight dangling crystals hung from her earlobes. A matching necklace graced her long neck.

Her purple sleeveless dress hugged all the right curves and fell just above her knees. Strappy high-heeled shoes accentuated her delicate ankles and sexy calves.

Beautiful.

Lucy was a small-town girl, but tonight she'd dressed for the big city. Whether this was a real date or not, she'd put some effort into getting ready. That pleased him.

"You look stunning."

She smiled softly. "I figured since we were going to Otto's…"

"Connor told you."

"Nine-year-olds and magpies have a lot in common," she explained. "So what did it cost you to enlist him and Marco as your partners in crime?"

Manny lumbered over toward the door. Lucy blocked his way so he couldn't get out of the house. The cat rubbed against her bare leg. Ryland wished he could do the same.

"Twenty bucks," he said, unrepentant.

Her mouth gaped. If this were a real date, he would have been tempted to take advantage of the moment and kiss her. But it wasn't, so he didn't.

"You paid the boys that much?" she asked.

He shrugged. "They earned it."

"Paying someone to do your dirty work gets expensive."

But worth every dollar. "A man does what he has to do."

"Even for a pretend date?" she said.

"A date's a date."

"That explains your clothes." Lucy's assessing gaze traveled the length of him. The brown chinos and green button-down shirt were the dressiest things he'd brought with him to Wicksburg. Going out hadn't been on his list of things to do here. "You clean up well."

He straightened, happy he'd pulled out all the stops tonight. "You sound surprised."

A half smile formed on her lips. "Well, I've only seen you in soccer shorts, jerseys and T-shirts."

Ryland remembered the first day she'd shown up at his parents' house. He raised a brow. "And shirtless."

Her cheeks turned a charming shade of pink. "That, too."

He handed her the iris. The color matched her dress perfectly. "For you."

"Thank you." She took the flower and smelled it. "It's real."

"Not everything is pretend."

She smiled. "I've always liked irises better than roses."

Score. "It reminded me of you."

Her eyes widened. "You don't have to say stuff like that. No one is watching us."

He held his hands up, his palms facing her. "Just being honest."

She kept staring at the flower. "Let me put this in some water before we go."

With an unexpected bounce to his step, Ryland entered the house and closed the door behind him. He followed Lucy, enjoying the sway of her hips and the flow of her dress around her legs. Her heels clicked against the floor. Manny trotted along behind him.

In the kitchen, she filled a narrow glass vase with water. She studied the flower, turning it 360 degrees, then stuck the stem into the vase. "I want to paint this."

Satisfaction flowed through him. "I'd like to see your work."

"We need to get to Otto's."

"There's no rush," he said. "I called the restaurant. No reservations unless it's a party of six or more."

She tilted her chin. "You're going to a lot of trouble for a pretend date."

"Connor doesn't want you to be lonely tonight."

"Connor, huh?"

Ryland's gaze met hers. Such pretty blue eyes. "I don't, either."

And that was the truth. Which surprised him a little. Okay, a lot. This was supposed to be all make-believe, but the more time he spent with Lucy, the more he cared about her. He wanted to make her smile and laugh. He wanted to please her.

This had never happened to him with a woman before. He wasn't sure what to think or even if he liked it.

Silence stretched between them, but if anything, the quiet drew them closer together not apart.

The sounds of the house continued on. Ice cubes dropped inside the freezer. A motor on the refrigerator whirred. Manny drank water from his bowl.

Funny, but Ryland had never felt this comfortable around anyone except his parents. He needed to figure out what was going on here. "So your paintings…"

"I'm really hungry."

So was Ryland. But what he wanted wasn't on any menu. She was standing right next to him. "Then let's go."

As Ryland held open the door to Otto's, Lucy walked into the restaurant. The din of customers talking and laughing rose above the accordion music playing. She inhaled the tantalizing aromas of roasting pork and herbs lingering in the air.

Her stomach rumbled. She'd been too nervous about the soccer game to eat lunch. Big mistake because now she was starving.

For food and for…

She glanced over her shoulder at Ryland. The green shirt lightened his hazel eyes. He looked as comfortable in dressier clothes as casual ones. He'd gone out of his way to make to-night special. She appreciated that even if none of this was for real. "Thanks for taking me out tonight."

"Thanks for going out with me."

Otto's was packed. Not surprising given it was a Saturday night and the best place in town. The last time she'd been here was right before Aaron and Dana deployed—a going away dinner for them.

Customers crammed into booths and tables. Servers carried heavy trays of German food and large steins full of beer. People waited to be seated. Some stood near the hostess stand. Others sat on benches.

Ryland approached the hostess, who was busy marking the seating chart. The woman in her early twenties looked up with a frown. But as soon as she saw him, a dazzling smile broke across her young, pretty face.

Lucy was beginning to realize wherever Ryland went female attention was sure to follow. But she saw he did nothing to make women come on to him. Well, except for being an extremely good-looking and all-around good guy. She stepped closer to him, feeling territorial. Silly considering this wasn't a real date.

"Hello. I'm Emily. Welcome to Otto's." She smoothed her hair. "How many in your party?"

"Two," he said.

She fluttered her eyelashes coquettishly. "Your name, please?"

"James."

The hostess wrote the information on her list. "You're looking at a thirty-minute wait, but I'll see what I can do."

Lucy was surprised the woman didn't ask for Ryland's phone number or hand him hers. More women, both staff and customers, stared at him.

He shot Lucy a sideward glance. "Half hour okay?"

"The cheese fondue is worth the wait."

Ryland raised a brow. "Even when you're hungry?"

"Especially then."

Other customers made their way out of the restaurant while more entered. He moved closer to her to make room in the small, crowded lobby area. "Connor told me how much you love the cheese fondue here."

"It's my favorite."

"Not chocolate?"

"Chocolate, cheese. I'm not that particular as long as it's warm and..."

"Gooey."

"Lucy?" a familiar male voice asked.

No. No. No. Every muscle in her body tensed. She squeezed her eyes shut in hopes she was dreaming, but when she opened them she was still standing in Otto's. Her ex-husband, Jeff Swanson, and his wife, Amelia, weaved through the crowd toward her. Jeff's receding hairline had gotten worse. And Amelia. She looked different…

Lucy narrowed her gaze for a better look.

Pregnant.

Pain gripped her chest. Life wasn't fair. She sighed.

Ryland stiffened. "You okay?"

"No." Not unless aliens were about to beam her up to the mother ship would she be okay. Being probed and prodded by extraterrestrials would be better than having to speak with the two people who had hurt her most. "But I'll survive."

At least she hoped so.

Jeff crowded in next to them. "I almost didn't recognize you."

The smell of his aftershave brought a rush of memories she'd rather forget. The bad times had overshadowed any good ones that might have existed at the beginning. "It's me."

"I see that now." Jeff's gaze raked over her. "But you cut your hair short. And you must have lost what? Twenty-five pounds or more?"

Stress had made eating difficult after the divorce. Going out solo or fixing a meal for one wasn't much fun, either. She'd also discovered Zumba classes at a nearby gym when she moved to Chicago. "Fifteen."

"Good for you," Amelia said. "It seems like we never stopped dieting when we were in high school. Remember that soup diet? I still can't stand the sight or smell of cabbage."

Until finding out about the affair, Lucy had been thankful to have Amelia for a best friend. Lucy had always felt inadequate, an ugly duckling compared to pretty Amelia with her jade-green eyes and shoulder-length blond hair. Amelia's hair now fell to her mid-back. Jeff liked long hair. That was why Lucy had chopped hers off.

Jeff extended his arm to shake hands. "Ryland James. I'm surprised to see you back in town."

His jaw tensed. "My parents still live here."

"Amelia, do you remember Ryland?" Jeff asked. "Soccer player extraordinaire."

"Of course." Amelia smiled sweetly. "Lucy had the biggest crush on you when we were in middle school."

"I know," Ryland said.

Lucy's heart went splat against the restaurant's hardwood floor. "You did?"

He nodded.

Aaron must have told Ryland. But why would her brother have done that? Her crush was supposed to be a secret.

"I didn't know," Jeff announced.

"Husbands." Amelia shook her head. "I mean, ex-husbands are always the last to know."

Ignore her. Ignore her. Ignore her.

Lucy repeated the mantra in her head so she didn't say anything aloud. The words wanting to come out of her mouth were neither ladylike nor appropriate for a public setting.

So what if she would have rather told Ryland about her failed marriage? Amelia was not worth causing a scene over.

Ryland put his arm around Lucy and pulled her against him. He toyed with her hair, wrapping a curl around his finger.

Her heart swelled with gratitude. She hated needing anyone. She'd been so weak when she'd been younger she wanted to be strong now that she was healthy. But she needed him at this moment.

She sunk against Ryland, soaking up his warmth and his strength, feeling his heart beat. The constant rhythm, the sound of life, comforted her.

Lucy smiled up at him.

He smiled back.

Both Jeff and Amelia stared with dumbfounded expressions on their faces.

Ryland had been right. Words weren't always necessary. People believed what they wanted, even if their assumptions might be incorrect.

Amelia's eyes darkened. She pressed her lips into a thin line.

Jeff's gaze bounced between Lucy and Ryland. "The two of you are...together?"

Lucy understood the disbelief in his voice. She and Ryland

made an unlikely pair, but still she nodded. She didn't like dishonesty after all the lies people had told her, but this didn't bother her so much. They were having dinner together tonight. Not the "together" Jeff had been talking about, but "together" nonetheless.

"I'd heard you were back in town taking care of Connor, but I had no idea about the two of you," Jeff said, not sounding pleased at all.

Good. Let him stew in his own cheating, miserable, arrogant juices.

Biting back a cutting retort, she glanced up at Ryland.

He kept playing with her hair with one hand while the other kept a possessive hold around her. His gaze held Lucy's for a long moment, the kind that elicited envious sighs from movie audiences. She'd owe him big-time for pretending like this, but she would gladly pay up.

"Soccer isn't that big in the U.S.," Ryland said. "But I played in the U.K. where the media coverage is insane so I try to keep a low profile with my personal life."

Amelia's face scrunched so much it looked painful. "But you're not staying here, are you? I thought you played on the West Coast somewhere."

"Phoenix." Ryland's gaze never wavered from Lucy's, making her insides feel all warm and gooey. "Though I wouldn't mind playing for Indianapolis so I could be closer to Wicksburg."

A thrill rushed through her. That was only a couple of hours away.

"We're having a baby," Amelia blurted as if no one had noticed her protruding belly. "It's a boy."

"Congratulations," both Lucy and Ryland said at the same time.

"I know how badly you wanted children when you were with Jeff," Amelia said to her. "Maybe something happened because of your liver. All those medicines you took and the transplant. But adoption is always an option."

After two years of trying to conceive, she hadn't been able to get pregnant. The doctors said there was no medical reason why she shouldn't be able to have a baby. Amelia knew that. So did Jeff. And it wasn't as if the two of them had gotten pregnant right away. Still feelings of inadequacy pummeled Lucy. Her shoulders slumped.

Ryland cuddled her close, making her feel accepted and special. "Kids aren't easy to handle. But you should see how great Lucy is with Connor."

Amelia patted her stomach. "Jeff and my best friend, Madison, are throwing me a baby shower. They've been planning it for weeks. I can't wait."

The words reminded Lucy of something she'd buried in the far recesses of her mind. Pain sliced through her, sharp and unyielding, at the betrayal of trust by Jeff and Amelia.

"I remember when the two of you spent all that time planning my birthday party." The words tasted bitter on Lucy's tongue. "That's when your affair started, right?"

Amelia gasped. She glared at a contrite-looking Jeff then stormed out of the restaurant.

"Damn." Jeff ran after her calling, "It's not what you think."

Lucy looked toward the door. "I almost feel sorry for her."

"Don't. She knew who and what she was marrying. Swanson is a complete moron." Ryland kept his arm around her. Lucy felt safe and secure in his embrace. His presence took the sting out of the past. "Any guy who would choose that woman over you doesn't have a brain cell in his head."

"Thanks," she said, grateful for his support in the face of her bad judgment. "But the truth is, I should have never married a guy like him."

"Why did you?" Ryland asked.

At a small table for two in the corner of the restaurant, candlelight glowed from a glass votive holder, creating a dancing circle against the white linen tablecloth. Ryland sat across from Lucy, their knees brushing against each other. A bowl of cheese fondue, a basket of bread cubes and a plate with two Bavarian Pretzels were between them.

As Lucy talked about Jeff Swanson, Ryland wished he could

change the past and erase the pain she'd experienced from her disastrous marriage.

"People warned me about Jeff." Lucy kept her chin up, her gaze forward, not downcast. But the hurt in her voice was unmistakable. "Told me to break up with him while we were dating. Aaron. Even Amelia. But I thought I knew better than all of them. I thought I could trust Jeff, but he had me so fooled."

"I doubt you're the only one he fooled."

She nodded. "After we eloped, I discovered Jeff hadn't been honest with me. He didn't like how independent and self-reliant I'd been while we were dating. He expected me to turn into his needy little wife. One who stayed home, cooked, cleaned and doted upon him. I admit I was far from the ideal spouse he expected. Amelia is more the doting type he wanted." Lucy stabbed her fork into a piece of bread. "But that didn't give him a reason to cheat."

"Jeff treated girls badly in high school, but they still wanted to go out with him."

She poked the bread again. "I don't think he knew I existed in high school. But when we bumped into each other in college, he laid on the charm. He knew what girls wanted to hear. At least what this girl needed to hear."

Her piece of bread had been stabbed so many times it was falling apart. He didn't think Lucy realized what she was doing with her appetizer fork. "There's not much left of that piece of bread. You might want to try another cube."

"Sorry." She stuck her fork into another piece and dipped the bread into the cheese. It fell into the pot. "I know I played a part in the breakup. It takes two people to make a marriage. But I wish Jeff had been more up-front and honest about what he wanted from me."

Ryland respected how she took responsibility, not laying all the blame on a cheating spouse. "If you could do it over…"

"I wouldn't," she said firmly. "I'm better off without him, but I'll admit it's hard being back in town. So many people know what happened. I'm sure they're pitying me the way they did when I was sick and talking behind my back."

"What people say doesn't matter." He wanted to see her smile, not look so sad. "Forget about them. Don't let it get to you. You're strong enough to do that."

"Strong?" Her voice cracked. "I'm a wimp."

"You came back to Wicksburg."

"Only because Aaron asked me," she admitted. "I couldn't have taken this leap on my own."

Damn Jeff Swanson. He'd not only destroyed Lucy's trust in others, but also in herself. "Give it time. Go slow."

She winced. "I'm trying. It's just when we were dating, Jeff made me feel…"

Ryland didn't want to push, but curiosity got the best of him. "What?"

Her gaze met his. The depth of betrayal in her eyes slammed into him, as if he'd run headfirst into the left goalpost. He reached across the table and laced his fingers with hers.

She took a deep breath and exhaled slowly. "You know about my liver transplant."

Ryland nodded.

"Someone died so I could live." Her tone stressed the awfulness of the situation and made him wondered if she somehow felt guilty. "I always wondered—I still wonder—whether that person's family would think I was living up to their expectations. I mean, their child's death is what enabled me to have the transplant. Given that ultimate sacrifice, would they be disappointed with what I've done with my life? What I'm doing or not doing now?"

Ryland's heart ached for her. That was a heavy load for anyone to carry. Especially someone as sensitive and sweet as Lucy. He squeezed her hand.

"Jeff's real appeal, I think, was that he made me believe we could achieve something big, something important together. With his help, I could prove I deserved a second chance with a new liver." Her mouth turned down at the corner. Angst clouded her eyes. "But we didn't. It was all talk. He no longer cared about that once we were married."

The sorrow in her voice squeezed Ryland's heart like a vice grip.

"I wanted to make a difference because of the gift I was given." Her mouth twisted with regret. "But I didn't do that when I was married to Jeff. I haven't done anything on my own, either. I doubt I ever will."

Her disappointment clawed at Ryland. "You're making a huge difference for Connor. For Aaron and his wife, too."

She shrugged. "But it's not something big, world changing."

"For your family it is." Did Lucy not know how special she was? "Look at yourself. You graduated college. You run your own business. That's a lot for someone your age."

"I'm twenty-six," she said with wry sarcasm. "Divorced. In debt with college loans and a car payment. I'm living at my brother's house, and all my possessions fit inside my car."

"You beat liver disease," Ryland countered. "Your being here—alive—is more than enough."

She stared at him as if she was trying to figure him out. A soft smile teased the corners of her mouth. "Where have you been all my life? Well, these past two years?"

Ryland was wondering the same thing. The realization should bother him more than it did.

"Thank you." Gratitude filled her eyes. Her appreciation wasn't superficial or calculated, but from her heart and made him feel valued. She squeezed his hand. "For tonight. For listening to me."

He stroked Lucy's hand with his thumb. "Thanks aren't necessary. I asked you to tell me. I've also been there myself."

Oops. Ryland hadn't meant to say that. He pulled his hand away and took a sip from his water glass.

She pinned him with a questioning gaze. "You?"

He tightened his grip on the glass, wanting to backpedal. "It's not the same. Not even close."

"I've spilled my guts," Lucy said. "It's your turn."

Ryland never opened up the way she had with him. People only valued him for what he could give them. If they knew him, the real him, they would think he wasn't worth much off the pitch. He took another sip of water then placed the glass on the table.

The tilt of her chin told him she wasn't going to let this drop. Of all the people in his life, Lucy didn't care about his fortune or fame. She had never asked him for anything for herself. She was always thinking of others. That included him. If he could tell anyone the truth, it was Lucy.

He swallowed around the emotion clogging his throat. "When I was in elementary school, I was bullied."

"Verbally?"

He nodded. "Sometimes…a lot of times…physically."

Lucy gasped. She placed her hand on top of his, the way he'd done with hers only moments before. "Oh, Ryland. I'm so sorry. That had to be horrible."

"Some days I felt invisible. As if kids were looking right through me." He'd never told anyone about this. Not even his parents. He thought telling Lucy would be hard, but the compassion in her eyes kept him going. "Those were the good days. Otherwise I would get pushed around, even beat up."

He'd felt like such a loser, a nobody, but he'd soon realized bullies were the real losers. Bullies like Jeff Swanson. Ryland would never tell Lucy her ex-husband had been one of the kids who terrorized students like him at Wicksburg Elementary School. That would only upset her more.

Concern knotted her brow. "I had no idea that went on."

"You were a little girl." He remembered her with ponytails and freckles playing hopscotch or swinging at recess. Seemingly without a care in the world. He hadn't known until later that she was so sick. "Some older kids like Aaron knew, but if they stood up to the bullies, they got beat up, too."

Her mouth formed a perfect O. "The time Aaron said he'd fallen off the monkey bars and gotten a black eye."

"One kid couldn't do much. Even a cool guy like your brother." Ryland remembered telling Aaron not to interfere but the guy wouldn't listen. "I hated going to school so much. I hated most everything back then. Except football. Soccer."

Lucy's smile filled him with warmth, a way he'd never felt

when thinking about this part of his past. "You found your passion at a young age."

"I liked being part of a team," he admitted. "It didn't matter that I lived in a dumpy apartment on the wrong side of town or was poor or got beat up all the time. When I put on that jersey, I fit in."

She squeezed his hand. "Thank goodness for soccer."

"It was my escape. My salvation." He took a sip of water. "With my teammates alongside me, the bullies had to leave me alone."

She smiled softly. "Your teammates took care of their star player."

He nodded. "Football gave me hope. A way out of Wicksburg so I could make something of myself. Be someone other than the scrawny kid who people picked on."

Kindness and affection reflected in her eyes. "You've done that. You've accomplished so much."

His chest tightened. She was one of a kind. "So have you."

Her hand still rested on his, making everything feel comfortable and natural. Right.

Ryland was in no hurry to have her stop touching him. He had no idea what was going on between them. Pretend, real... He didn't care.

Slowly, almost reluctantly, Lucy pulled her hand away. "Wicksburg holds some bad memories for both of us."

He missed her softness and her warmth. "Some good ones, too."

Like the memories they were creating right now.

She tried to pull the lost bread cube out of the fondue bowl. "At first I wasn't sure about us pretending to date. I don't like being dishonest. But after seeing Jeff and Amelia, I'm thankful you were with me tonight. I know this is what's best for Connor. And the only way for you to help the team."

"And help you."

"And me."

"We're not being that dishonest," he said. "If you think about it, what we're doing is kind of like the funeral."

Her eyes widened. "Funeral?"

Lucy reminded him of Connor. "Playacting at Squiggy's funeral."

She laughed. "You mean his first funeral. Not the top-secret one I wasn't supposed to know about."

Ryland smiled at her lighthearted tone. "Now this is more like it. No more being upset over an idiot like Jeff. It's time for laughter and fun."

"That's exactly what I need."

She raised the piece of fondue-covered bread to her mouth. Her lips closed around it.

So sexy. Ryland's temperature soared. He took another sip of water. Too bad she also didn't need some kisses.

A drop of cheese remained at the corner of her mouth. Ryland wished he could lick it off. "You have a little cheese on your mouth."

She wiped with a napkin, but missed the spot.

Reaching across the table, he used his thumb to remove the cheese, ignoring how soft her lips looked or how badly he wanted to taste their sweetness again. "It's gone."

Her eyes twinkled with silver sparks. "Thanks."

Lucy wouldn't be thanking him if she knew what he was thinking. "You're welcome."

The server arrived with their main courses. Sauerbraten, spatzle noodles and braised red cabbage for Lucy. Jagerschnitzel with mashed potatoes for him. The food smelled mouthwateringly delicious.

As they ate, Ryland couldn't stop thinking about what would happen after dinner and dessert were finished. When it was the two of them back at her house. Alone. This might be a pretend date, but he wanted to kiss her good-night.

For real.

CHAPTER TEN

RIDING in the old, blue truck, Lucy glanced at Ryland, who sat next to her on the bench seat. With his chiseled good looks, his handsome profile looked as if it had been sculpted, especially with the random headlights casting shadows on his face. But there was nothing hard and cold about the man. He was generous, caring and funny. He might be portrayed as being a bad boy in the press, but she'd glimpsed the man underneath the façade and liked what she saw.

He turned onto the street where she lived.

After spilling secrets, she and Ryland had spent the rest of dinner laughing over jokes, stories and memories. Too bad the evening had to end.

"I can't believe we ate that entire apple strudel after all the fondue and dinner," she said.

"We," he teased. "I only had two bites."

"More like twenty-two."

He parked at the curb and set the gear. "Math's never been a strong point. Which is why soccer is the perfect sport for me. Scores rarely reach two digits."

She grinned. "That's why they invented calculators. For all us right-brained people who can't tell the difference between Algebra and Calculus."

"What about addition and subtraction?" With a wink, he removed the key from the ignition. "Stay there. I'll get the door for you."

His manners impressed Lucy. Okay, she may have assumed

athletes had more in common with Neanderthals than gentle-
men, but Ryland was proving her wrong. About many things
tonight.

The passenger door opened. He extended his arm. "Milady?"

Lucy didn't need Ryland's help, but accepted it anyway. He
wasn't offering because she was incapable or unhealthy. He was
doing this to be polite. She would gladly play along. "Thank
you, kind sir."

The touch of her fingers against his skin caused a spark.
Static electricity from the truck's carpet? Whatever it was, heat
traveled through her, igniting a fire she hadn't felt in a long
time and wasn't sure what to do with.

As soon as she was out of the truck and standing on the sidewalk, Ryland let go of her. A relief, given her reaction, but she
missed his touch.

"You must be cold," he said.

Even with the cool night air and her sleeveless dress, she
wasn't chilly. Not with Ryland next to her.

"I'm fine." Thousands of stars twinkled overhead. She'd forgotten what the night sky looked like in the country compared
to that in a city. "It's a beautiful night."

"Very beautiful."

She glanced his way.

He was looking at her, not the sky. Her body buzzed with
awareness. She could stand out here with him all night.

His smile crinkled the corners of his eyes and did funny
things to her heart rate.

Tearing her gaze away, Lucy headed up the paved walkway
toward the front porch. Ryland followed her, his steps sounding against the concrete.

Uncertainty coursed through Lucy. Ryland made her feel
so special tonight, listening in a way Jeff never had and sharing a part of himself with her.

This wasn't a real date. Except at some point this evening,
she hadn't been pretending. Ryland hadn't seemed to be, either. That...worried her.

Lucy didn't trust herself when it came to men, especially

Ryland. Best to say a quick good-night and make a hasty re-treat inside. Alone. So she could figure this out.

On the porch, she reached into her purse with a shaking hand and pulled out her keys. "I had a great time. Thanks."

"The night's still young."

Anticipation revved her blood. She wanted to invite him in. Who was she kidding? She wanted to throw herself into his arms and kiss him until they ran out of air. Or the sun came up.

Lucy couldn't deny the flush of desire, but if they started something would she be able to stop? Would she want to stop? To go too far would be disastrous. "I'm thinking we should call it a night."

He ran his finger along her jawline. "You think?"

Lucy gulped. "I'm not ready for taking any big leaps."

"What about a small one?"

His lips beckoned. Hers ached. Maybe just a little kiss...

She lifted her chin and kissed him on the mouth. Hard.

Ryland pressed his mouth against Lucy's with a hunger that matched her own. He wrapped his arms around her, pulling her closer. She went eagerly, arching against him. This was what she wanted...needed.

The keys dropped from her fingers and clattered on the step. She placed her hands on his shoulders, feeling the ridges of his muscles beneath her fingertips.

His lips moved over hers. She parted her lips, allowing their tongues to explore and dance.

Pleasurable sensations shot through her. She clung to him and his kiss. Longing pooled low in her belly. A moan escaped her lips.

Ryland drew the kiss to an end. "Wow."

That pretty much summed it up. She took a breath and an-other. It didn't help. Her breathing was still ragged. And her throbbing lips...

She fought the urge to touch them to see that what she'd ex-perienced hadn't been a dream. "I've been trying to curb my impulsive side. Looks like I failed."

"I'd give you an A+ and recommend letting yourself be more impulsive." Wicked laughter lit his eyes. He kept his arms around her. "We could go inside and see where our impulses take us."

Most likely straight into the bedroom. Lucy's heart slammed against her chest.

A sudden fear dampened her desire. She'd been hurt too badly, didn't trust her judgment or the feelings coursing through her right now. Especially with a man who had more opportunity to cheat than her ex-husband ever had.

Ryland James is a player, Luce. He'll break your heart if he gets the chance.

Aaron's words echoed through her head. "We can't. I mean, I can't."

Ryland combed his fingers through her hair. "If you think I'm pretending, I'm not."

"Me, either." Her resolve weakened. "But I have to think of Connor."

"He's spending the night with Marco."

Her mouth went dry with the possibilities. "You're leaving town soon."

"True, but we can make the most of the time I have left," Ryland said, his voice husky and oh-so tempting. "You said you didn't want a boyfriend. I'm not looking for a girlfriend."

"Not a real one at least."

"Touché."

"This has nowhere to go. I'm not up for a fling. Aaron thinks if we get involved, you'll break my heart."

Ryland stiffened. "Your brother said that?"

"The other night when he called."

His mouth quirked. "So let's just keep doing what we've been doing."

"Pretending."

"We'll date, but keep it light," he said. "No promises. No guarantees."

"No sex."

"You've made that clear." He sounded amused, not upset. "Except how do you feel about pretend sex?"

"Huh?"

"Never mind," he said. "We'll just have fun and enjoy each other's company until it's time for me to go back to Phoenix."

Lucy wasn't one to play with fire. She'd done everything in her power these past two years to keep from getting burned again. But this was different. She knew where she stood with Ryland. He'd been honest with her. They could make this work. But she would keep a fire extinguisher handy in case the flames got out of control. Getting burned was one thing. She didn't want to wind up a pile of ash. "Okay. We can keep doing what we've been doing."

On Sunday afternoon, Ryland knocked on Lucy's front door. He'd done the same thing less than twenty-four hours ago. But he felt more anticipation today.

She'd been on his mind since last night. Her kisses had fueled his fantasies, making him want more.

But she wasn't ready to give more. At least not the more he wanted.

I don't sleep around.

I'm not up for a fling.

No sex.

She hadn't said anything about no kisses. He'd settle for those. Maybe Lucy would change her mind about the physical part of their…not relationship…hanging out.

The front door opened. Connor smiled up at him with a toothy grin. "Fuego plays in an hour."

This was the second game of the season for his team. They were in L.A. to play against the Galaxy. Ryland had missed not being at the season opener earlier this week when the team lost to the Portland Timbers. He'd felt like he was letting down his teammates and fans down being unable to play. He looked at his foot.

The orthopedist had told Ryland he might get the boot off in another week or two. That meant he would be able to return to the team, but in order to do that he would have to leave Wicksburg.

Wait a minute. Leaving town would be a good thing. Nothing was holding him here. Well, except his parents who would be returning home this week.

And Lucy. But he couldn't let himself go there. When he could play again, soccer would have to be his total focus. He couldn't afford any distractions. She would be a big one.

"Aunt Lucy told me to cheer loudly." Connor grabbed Manny who was darting between his legs, trying get out of the house. "I have to finish my math homework first. Aunt Lucy said so."

"Better get to it, bud." Ryland entered the house. He closed the door behind him. "I don't want to watch the game without you."

Connor ran off to his bedroom to finish his homework. Ryland walked to the kitchen.

The scents of cheese and bacon filled the air. His mouth watered, as much for whatever was baking as the woman unloading the dishwasher. Lucy wore a pair of jean shorts. Her T-shirt inched up in the back showing him a flash of ivory skin in the back as she bent over to grab silverware. Her lime V-neck T-shirt gaped revealing the edge of her white-lace bra.

Beautiful.

He stepped behind and wrapped his arms around Lucy. Her soft-in-all-the-right-places body fit perfectly against his. Knowing they were alone while Connor did his math, Ryland showered kisses along her jawline.

She faced him. Silver sparks flashed in her eyes. "Is this how you normally say hello?"

"No, I prefer this way."

He lowered his mouth to hers. His lips soaked in her warmth and sweetness. His heart rate tripled. The blood rushed from his head.

She arched against him, taking the kiss deeper. He followed her lead, relieved she was as into kissing as he was. He liked kissing Lucy. He wanted to keep on kissing her.

Forever.

Ryland jerked back.

He didn't do forever.

She stared up at him with flushed cheeks and swollen lips. The passion in her eyes matched the desire rushing through his veins. Definitely a keeper. If he was looking for one...

Lucy grinned. "I like how you say hello."

He liked it, too. Especially with her.

But he had to remember to keep things light. No thoughts about forever. They had two weeks, if they were lucky. No reason to get carried away.

And he wouldn't. That wouldn't be fair to Lucy. Or her brother.

He owed Aaron that much, even if his old friend was wrong about Ryland breaking Lucy's heart. He wouldn't do that to her.

He inhaled. "Whatever you're cooking smells delicious."

"Macaroni and cheese." She turned on the oven light so he could see the casserole dish baking inside. "Dana marked her cookbooks with Connor's favorite recipes."

"I smell bacon."

Lucy smiled coyly. "That's one of the secret ingredients."

"I didn't know you were allowed to divulge secret ingredients."

She shrugged. "We shared our secrets last night so I figured why not."

The vase containing the iris he'd given her sat on the counter. Paintbrushes dried alongside it. "If we have nothing left to hide, show me your paintings."

Her lips quirked. "You really want to see them?"

She sounded surprised by his interest in her art. "I do, or I wouldn't keep asking."

"I—I don't show my work to a lot of people."

"It's just me."

Uncertainty flickered in her eyes. "Exactly."

Ryland didn't understand what she meant. "Show me one."

She raised a brow. "That'll be enough to appease your curiosity?"

He wasn't sure of anything when it came to Lucy. But he

would take what he could get. "Yes. I'll leave it up to you if you want to show me more."

She glanced at the oven timer. "I suppose we have time now."

Not the most enthusiastic response, but better than a no. "Great."

Lucy led him down a hallway covered with framed photographs. One picture showed a large recreational vehicle that looked more like a bus.

"Is that your parents' RV?" he asked.

"Yes," she said. "How did you know about that?"

"Connor told me his grandparents were living in a camper and traveling all over the country."

"Yes, that's how they dreamed of spending their retirement. They finally managed to do it three months ago." She peeked in on Connor, who sat at his desk doing his homework. "They're in New Mexico right now."

Ryland wondered what Lucy dreamed of doing. He considered asking, but any of her dreams would be on hold until Aaron and his wife returned. Ryland admired Lucy's sacrifice. He'd thought watching Cupcake had been a big deal. Not even close. He followed her through another doorway.

The bedroom was spotless with nothing out of place. The queen-size bed, covered with a flower-print comforter and matching pillow shams, drew his attention. This was where Lucy slept. Alone, but the bed was big enough for two.

Don't even think about it. He looked away.

She went to the closet.

Ryland knew what to expect from a typical twenty-something woman's closet—overflowing with clothing, shoes and purses.

Lucy opened the door.

Only a few clothing items hung on the rack. A sheet of plastic covered the closet floor. Five pairs of shoes sat on top. Not a handbag in sight. Instead, the backsides of different-size canvases and boxes of art supplies filled the space.

Not typical at all.

Given this was Lucy he shouldn't have been surprised.

"This is something I painted when I was living in Chicago."

As she reached for the closest painting, her hand trembled.

Ryland touched her shoulder. He wanted to see her work, but he didn't want to make her uncomfortable. Her bare skin felt soft and warm beneath his palm. "We can do this another time."

"Now is fine." She glanced back at him. "It's just a little hard…"

"To show this side of yourself."

She nodded.

The vulnerability in her eyes squeezed his heart. Her affect on him unnerved Ryland. He lowered his arm from her shoulder. "If it's any consolation, I know nothing about art. I'm about as far removed from an art critic as you can get."

"So if you like it, I'll remember not to get too excited."

He smiled.

She smiled back.

His heart stumbled over itself. His breath rushed from his lungs as if he'd played ninety minutes without a break at half-time.

What was going on?

All she'd done was smile. Something she'd done a hundred times before. But he could hardly breathe.

She pulled out the canvas. "Ready?"

No. Feeling unsteady, he sat on the bed.

"Sure." He forced the word from his tight throat.

Lucy turned the canvas around.

Ryland stared openmouthed and in awe. He'd expected to see a bowl of fruit or a bouquet of flowers. Not a vibrant, colorful portrait full of people having fun. The painting depicted a park with people picnicking, riding bicycles, pushing baby strollers and flying kites.

A good thing he was sitting or he would have fallen flat on his butt. The painting was incredible. Amazing. He felt transported, as if he were in the park seeing what she'd seen, feeling what she'd felt. Surreal.

He took a closer look. "Is that guy eating a hot dog?"

She nodded. "What's a day in the park without a hot dog from a vendor?"

Drops of yellow mustard dripped onto the guy's chin and shirt. The amount of detail amazed Ryland. He noticed a turtle painted next to the pond. An homage to Squiggy? "You're so talented."

"You know nothing about art," she reminded him.

"True, but I know quality when I see it," he said. "This is a thousand times better than any of the junk hanging on my walls in Phoenix."

She raised a brow. "I doubt those artists would consider their work junk."

He waved a hand. "You know what I mean."

"Thank you."

"No, thank you." This painting told him so much about Lucy. He could see her in each stroke, each character, each detail. Life exploded from the canvas. The importance of community, too. "I know a couple of people who own art galleries."

Her lips pursed. "Thanks, but I'm not ready to do that."

"You're ready," he encouraged. "Trust yourself. Your talent."

"I don't think I should do anything until Aaron and Dana get home."

Ryland hated to see Lucy holding back like this. "Think about it."

"I will. Would you like to see another one?" she asked to his surprise. "Not all of them are so cheery as this one. I went through a dark stage."

"Please." Looking at her work was like taking a peek inside her heart and her soul. He wanted to see more, as many paintings as she allowed him to see. "Show me."

Lucy would have never thought the best date ever would include mac and cheese, her nine-year-old nephew and a televised soccer game, but it had tonight. At first she'd been so nervous about showing Ryland her work, afraid of exposing herself like that and what he might think. He not only liked her paintings, but also understood them. Catching details most people overlooked.

She stood at the doorway to her nephew's bedroom while Ryland, by request, tucked Connor into bed.

The two talked about the game. Even though Fuego lost 0–1 to the Galaxy, both agreed it was a good game.

"They would have won if you'd been there," Connor said.

Ryland ruffled Connor's hair. "We'll never know."

"I can't wait to see you play."

As the soccer talk continued, Lucy leaned against the hallway wall.

Thanks to Ryland, her nephew was a happy kid again. Connor still missed his parents, but a certain professional soccer player had made a big difference. At least for now.

Lucy wondered if Connor realized when Ryland could play again he wouldn't be coaching. But if the Fuego played the Indianapolis Rage, maybe they could get tickets. She would have to check the match schedule.

Seeing Ryland play in person might be just the ticket to keep a smile on her nephew's face. Lucy had to admit she would like that, too.

"Good night, Connor." Ryland turned off the light in the bedroom. "I'll see you at practice tomorrow."

"'Night."

In the hallway, he laced his fingers with hers and led her into the living room. "I finally have you all to myself."

"We don't have to watch the post-match commentary?" she teased.

"I set the DVR so I wouldn't have to subject you to that." He pulled her against him. "But I will subject you to this."

Ryland's lips pressed against hers. His kiss was soft. Tender. Warm.

She leaned against him, only to find herself swept up in his arms. But his lips didn't leave hers.

He carried her to the couch and sat with her on his lap. Lucy wrapped her arms around him. Her breasts pressed against his hard chest.

As she ran her hands along his muscular shoulders and wove her fingers through her hair, she parted her lips. She wanted more of his kisses, more of him.

The pressure of his mouth against hers increased, full of hunger and heat. Her insides felt as if they were melting.

Ryland might be a world-class soccer player, but he was a world-class kisser, too.

Pleasurable sensations shot through her. Tingles exploded. If she'd been confused about the definition of chemistry, she understood it now.

Thank goodness he had his arms around her or she'd be falling to the floor, a mass of gooey warmth. Not that she was complaining. She clung to him, wanting even more of his kisses.

Slowly Ryland loosened his hold on her and drew the kiss to an end. "Told you this would be fun."

"You did." A good thing he wasn't going to be around long enough or this could become habit forming. Her chest tightened.

Lucy couldn't afford for anything about Ryland to become habit. She couldn't allow herself to get attached.

Neither of them was in a place to pursue a relationship. Neither of them could commit to anything long-term.

This was about spending time together in the short-term and having fun. And sharing some very hot kisses.

That had to be enough. Even if a part of her was wishing there could be...more.

CHAPTER ELEVEN

As the days passed, the temperature warmed. The sun stayed out longer. The Defeeters won more games than they lost. But Lucy wasn't looking forward to the end of spring. She didn't want Ryland to leave.

Being with him was exciting. Wicksburg no longer seemed like a boring, small town as they made the most of their time together. Practice twice a week. Dinner with Connor. Lunch when her work schedule or his physical therapy allowed. When she was alone, her painting flourished with heightened senses and overflowing creativity.

After Mr. and Mrs. James returned from their vacation, they became fixtures at games and invited everyone to dinner following a practice.

That Monday evening, a bird chirped in a nearby cherry tree in the Jameses' backyard. The cheery tune fit perfectly with the jubilant mood. The boys kicked a soccer ball on the grass while Cupcake chased after them barking.

Standing on the patio, Lucy watched the boys play.

"Connor reminds me of his father," Mrs. James said. She wore her salt-and-pepper hair in a ponytail, a pair of jeans and a button-down blouse. "Though he's a little taller than Aaron was at this age."

"Connor's mom is tall." Lucy glanced at Mrs. James. "Thank you for having us over tonight."

"Our pleasure. It's so nice to have children here." She stared at the boys running around. "I've been telling Ryland to settle down so I can have grandchildren to spoil, but that boy has only one thing on his mind."

"Soccer," Lucy said at the same time as his mother.

Mrs. James eyed her curiously. "You know him well."

Lucy shifted her weight between her feet. "He's been helping me with the team."

"And going out with you." Mrs. James smiled. "Hard to keep things secret in a town Wicksburg's size."

They hadn't tried hiding anything. The more people who knew they were going out, the better. Lucy wanted nothing more than to enjoy her time with Ryland, but she felt as if she was trying to hold on to the wind. He would be blowing out of her life much too soon.

"It's so nice Ryland is with someone who knew him before he became famous," Mrs. James said.

"He was always a star player around here."

Ryland shouted something to the boys. Laughter filled the air.

"Yes, but he thinks of himself as a footballer, nothing else," Mrs. James explained. "Ryland needs to realize that there's a life for him off the pitch, too. I hope being here and getting reacquainted with you and others will help him see that."

"Soccer is his only priority." Lucy had been reminding herself that for days now. All the smiles, laughter and kisses they shared would be coming to an end. But she didn't want to turn into a sighing lump because he was leaving. "He's not interested in anything else."

"I wonder if soccer would be as important to him if he thought there was somewhere else he belonged."

I liked being part of a team. It didn't matter that I lived in a dumpy apartment on the wrong side of town or was poor or got beat up all the time. When I put on that jersey, I fit in.

Lucy remembered what he'd told her. "Belonging is important to him, but Ryland doesn't think he belongs in Wicksburg."

Mrs. James's eyes widened. "You've talked about this?"

Lucy hoped she wasn't opening a can of worms for Ryland, but his mother seemed genuinely concerned. "A little."

"That's a start." Mrs. James's green eyes twinkled with pleasure. "It's going to take Ryland time to realize where he belongs, and that he's more than he thinks he is."

"Maybe when he gets back to Phoenix." Lucy's chest tightened. "He doesn't have much time left here."

"He can always come back."

Lucy nodded. She hoped Ryland would return after the MLS season ended, but that was months away.

"Well, I'd better finish getting the taco bar ready," Mrs. James said. "The boys must be starving."

"What can I do to help?" Lucy asked.

"Enjoy yourself."

As Mrs. James walked away, Cheryl came up. She held an iPad. "Getting on the mother's good side is smart. I should have done that with my mother-in-law."

"It's not too late," Lucy said.

"Well, the divorce papers haven't been filed yet. But I don't want to talk about my sorry situation." Cheryl showed Lucy an article from a U.K. tabloid's website. "Guess this is what happens when you're with one of the hottest footballers around."

Lucy stared at the iPad screen full of pictures of her and Ryland. "Why would they do this?"

Cheryl sighed. "Because it's so romantic."

Romantic, perhaps. But not…real. The photos made it appear as if Lucy and Ryland were falling for each other. Falling hard.

The top photograph was from the Defeeters' first game when Ryland kneeled behind her and whispered in her ear, but it looked as if he were kissing her neck. The second showed them in a booth at the pizza parlor sitting close together and gazing into each other's eyes. The last one captured their quick congratulatory peck after the team's first win, but the photograph made it seem like a long, tongue shoved down each other's throats full-on make-out session. Okay, they'd had a couple of those, but not where anyone could see them let alone take a picture.

As Lucy read the article, the blood rushed from her head.

The world spun. The pictures didn't imply a serious relationship. The words suggested an imminent engagement.

Oh, no. This was bad. "I can't believe this."

"I didn't realize things were so serious."

"Me, neither." Ryland wasn't going to like this. Lucy reread a paragraph. "They call me a WAG. Is that a British euphemism for hag or something?"

Cheryl laughed. "WAG stands for Wives and Girlfriends. Many women aspire to be one."

The acronym wasn't accurate. Surprisingly the thought of being Ryland's girlfriend didn't sound so bad. Unease slithered down Lucy's spine. She knew better to think that way. Dating Ryland didn't include being his girlfriend. Except everyone reading the article... "I hope people don't believe all this."

"You and Ryland care about each other. That's all that matters."

Care.

Yes, Lucy cared about Ryland. She cared...a lot.

As she stared at one of the photographs, a deeper attraction and affection for Ryland surfaced, accompanied by a sinking feeling in her stomach.

Oh, no. She'd been ignoring and pretending certain feelings didn't exist, but the article was bringing all that emotion out. She couldn't deny the truth any longer.

Lucy didn't just care about Ryland.

I love him.

The truth hit her like a gallon of paint dropped on her head. She'd fallen in love with Ryland James. Even though she'd known all the reasons why she shouldn't.

Stupid, stupid, stupid.

"You look pale," Cheryl said. "Are you okay?"

"I don't know," Lucy admitted. "I really don't know."

Ryland had pursued her. She'd pretended she couldn't be caught, but she'd been swept up by his charm and heart the minute he'd turned them on her.

Lucy wanted people to be honest with her, but she'd lied to

herself about how safe it was to date Ryland, to hang out with him, to kiss him.

"Don't let a gossip column bother you. Talk to Ryland about it," Cheryl suggested. "I'm sure he's dealt with this before."

Gossip, yes. But Lucy wasn't sure how many women had fallen in love with him. She couldn't imagine being the first, but she wasn't sure she wanted to know the number of women who had gone down this same path.

Talk to Ryland about it.

She'd experienced a change of heart about wanting a relationship. Maybe he'd had one, too. And if not...

No. This wasn't a crush. Her feelings weren't one-sided. His kisses were proof of that as was his wanting to spend time with her. He had feelings for her. She knew he did.

Lucy had shared her secrets and art with him. How hard could it be to tell him she'd lost her heart to him, too?

She would talk to Ryland and see where their feelings took them.

After dinner, Ryland carried in the leftovers from the taco bar while a soccer match between kids and adults was being fought to determine bragging rights.

In the kitchen, he set the pan of ground beef on the counter. "That's the last of it."

His mother handed him a plastic container. "I like Lucy."

"So do I."

"Good, because it's about time you got serious with a woman."

Ryland flinched. He stared at his mom in disbelief. "Who said anything about getting serious?"

"Your father and I aren't getting any younger. We'd like grandkids while we can still get around and play with them. You and Lucy would have cute babies."

"Whoa, Mom." Ryland held up his hands, as if that could stop a runaway train like his mom. "I like Lucy. That's a long way from having babies with her. I need to focus on my career."

His mom shrugged. "A soccer ball won't provide much comfort after you retire."

He spooned the meat into the container. "I'll settle down once I stop playing."

"That's years away."

Ryland covered the ground beef with a lid. "I hope so."

"That's not what your mother wants to hear."

"It's the truth," he admitted. "If I put down any kind of roots, I'm not going to be able to finish out my career the way I want to."

"A woman like Lucy won't wait around forever. She won't have to in a town like Wicksburg." His mom filled a plastic Ziploc baggie with the leftover shredded cheese. "While you're off playing football and partying with WAG wannabes, another man will sweep Lucy off her feet. She'll have a ring on her finger before Christmastime."

Ryland clenched his hands. Wait a minute. His mom had no idea what she was saying. "Lucy doesn't want a ring. Not from me or anyone else."

"You sound confident."

"I am," he admitted. "We talked about it."

"It?"

"Relationships. Lucy and I are on the same page." He wished his mom wasn't sticking her nose into his business. He kept his social life private so she wouldn't know what was going on. "I can't be thinking about a relationship right now because of soccer. Lucy doesn't want to be entangled by any guy while she's taking care of Connor."

His mom studied him. "So when you go back to Phoenix…"

"It's over."

"And when you come back?"

"You and Dad can visit me," Ryland said. "I've worked too hard to get out of Wicksburg."

"You ran away."

"I left to play soccer."

His mother took a deep breath then exhaled slowly. "You're an adult and capable of making your own decisions, but please, honey, think about what you may be giving up if you leave town, leave Lucy, and never look back."

He picked up the container of meat and placed it in the refrigerator. "You're way off base here, Mom."

"Maybe I am, but one of these days you're going to realize soccer isn't the only thing in the world. I'd like for you to have a life outside the game in place when that happens."

"You just want me back in Wicksburg raising a bunch of kids."

"I want you to be happy."

"I am happy." So what if a lot of his happiness right now had to do with Lucy? Their dating was only for the short-term. They both agreed. His mother was wrong. This was for the best. "I know what I'm doing. I know what I want."

And that didn't include Wicksburg or...Lucy.

Later that evening, after everyone had left, Lucy sat with Ryland on his parents' patio. Mr. James was showing Connor his big-screen TV while Mrs. James gave Cupcake a bath after the dog jumped into a garbage can.

Ryland leaned back in his chair. "The boys enjoyed themselves."

"Their parents, too." Lucy had thrown herself into playing soccer. A way to put a game face on, perhaps?

"Cheryl showed me an article from a U.K. tabloid tonight." Lucy held up the display screen of her smartphone. "It's about... us."

Heaven help her, but she liked saying the word "us." Ryland had to see how good they were together.

He took the phone and used his finger to scroll through the words. "This happens all the time. Don't let it bother you."

He sounded so nonchalant about the whole thing. "You don't mind that total strangers halfway across the globe are reading about us?"

"It's not about minding." As Ryland laced his fingers with hers, tingles shot up her arm. "Football is almost like a religion in other countries. Fans follow their favorite players' every move. If someone tweets that a star player is at the supermarket buying groceries, hundreds of people might show up in minutes. This article is no different than others they've published about me and other players."

"But you don't play over there anymore."

"I did," he said. "I could go back someday."

So far away. Lucy felt a pang in her heart. She didn't want him to leave. Not to Phoenix. Not anywhere.

She took a deep breath to calm her nerves. "The article makes it read like we're seriously dating, practically engaged."

"But we're not."

Ryland sounded so certain. No hesitation. No regret.

Lucy searched his face for a sign that he'd had a change of heart like her, but she saw nothing. Absolutely nothing to suggest he felt or wanted...more.

That frustrated her. She wanted him to be her boyfriend. The guy should want her to be his girlfriend.

Ryland put his arm around her. "This can be hard to deal with when you're not used to it. But it's how the game is played. You have to ignore it."

Lucy didn't want to ignore it. She wanted the article to be true. She wanted to be a WAG. Ryland's WAG. Not only his girlfriend, she realized with a start. But his...wife.

Mrs. Ryland James.

Lucy suppressed a groan. This was bad. Horrible. Tragic. *No promises. No guarantees. No sex.*

"Hey, don't be sad." Ryland caressed her face with his hand. "It's just a stupid article full of gossip and lies. Nothing to worry about."

His words were like jabs with a pitchfork to Lucy's heart. The more he downplayed the article, the more it bothered her. And hurt.

Irritation burned. At Ryland. At herself.

Forget about telling him how she felt. She wasn't going to give him the satisfaction of knowing how much she cared about him when he didn't or wouldn't admit how he felt about her.

Annoyed at the situation and at him, she raised her chin.

"I'm not worried. I just wanted to make sure this wouldn't damage the Ryland James brand."

The next day, Ryland took Cupcake on a walk around the neighborhood without the boot per his doctor's orders. He'd chosen this time because he knew Lucy had a call with a client and wouldn't see him.

He didn't know what was going on with her. She'd given off mixed signals last night. Her good-night kiss suggested she was into him. But her attitude about the tabloid article made him think she might be getting tired of him and unsettled by that side of his fame.

Ryland didn't know what her reaction to his getting the boot off would be.

The little gray dog ran ahead, pulling against the leash.

"Are you ready for me to go back to Phoenix, Cupcake?"

The dog ignored him and sniffed a bush.

"I'm not." He had to leave, but what he and Lucy had together was going to be hard to give up. More time with Lucy would be nice. More than nice. Too bad he couldn't go there or anywhere on the other side of nice. "But I'm not going to have a choice."

His cell phone rang. He pulled it from his pocket and glanced at the touch screen. Blake. About time. Ryland had left him a message last night.

"Did you plant the story about me and Lucy?" he asked.

"Hello to you, too." Blake sounded amused. "Yes, I'm doing well. Thanks for asking."

Ryland watched Cupcake sniff a patch of yellow and pink flowers. "Was it you?"

"No," Blake admitted. "That's not to say I didn't have a suggestion for the person who did."

Ryland knew it. The PR firm had to be involved. But Blake would never give him firm details. At least he hadn't in the past when something like this occurred. "Why?"

"Your future with Fuego isn't a sure thing," he said. "A serious girlfriend will help your image. Bad Boy Ryland James getting serious with a hometown girl. It sends the message you're maturing and getting out of the party scene."

Ryland pulled Cupcake away from a rose bush with thorns. "You're reaching for something that isn't there."

"I spoke with both your coach and Fuego's owner," Blake said. "Settling down is the best thing you can do right now."

"You're sounding a lot like my mom."

"Your mom's a smart woman."

Ryland looked around to see if anyone was on the street. Empty. "Lucy and I aren't serious."

"A big, sparkling diamond engagement ring from Tiffany & Co. will change all that."

He felt a flash of something, almost a little thrill at the thought of proposing to Lucy. Must be a new form of nausea. "Yeah, right. I'll catch a flight to Chicago tonight and go buy one."

"Indianapolis is closer," Blake said. "They have a store there according to their website."

"You're joking, right? Otherwise you've lost your mind."

"You said you wanted to play in the MLS," he said. "I'm making that happen for you."

"By lying."

"It's called stretching the truth," Blake said. "Let people see you buy an engagement ring. They can make their own assumptions."

"Lucy would never go for something like this."

"She'll be thrilled. Anyone who looks at those photographs can tell she's as crazy about you as you are about her."

"Crazy, maybe. But not in…" Ryland couldn't bring himself to say the word. "I like her." A lot. More than he'd ever thought possible. "But that doesn't mean I'm ready to get…serious."

Okay, so he'd thought about summer break and time off when he could be with Lucy and Connor. And Manny, the fat cat, too.

But Ryland had realized doing anything more than thinking about the future was stupid. He needed to focus, to prove himself, to play…

"Her life is in Wicksburg. At least as long as she's taking care of Connor," Ryland said. "My life is in Phoenix."

"You don't sound so excited about that anymore."

"I am." Wasn't he? Of course, he was. All this was messing with his head. "But Lucy can't spend the next year or so with us traveling back and forth between here and there, to see each other."

"You can afford it."

"Blake."

"Just playing devil's advocate."

"Be my advocate. That's what I pay you for."

"What do you want?"

Lucy. No, that wasn't possible. "I want to play again. Not the way I played last season with the Fuego, but the way I played over in the Premier League. When it…mattered to me. Working with the kids and Lucy reminded me how much I love the game. And how much I miss it."

"You don't sound the same as you did a month ago." Emotion filled Blake's voice. "For the first time in two years, it sounds like the real Ryland James is back."

"Damn straight, I am." But he couldn't get too excited. Thinking about leaving Lucy left a football-size hole in his chest.

But what could Ryland do? He had a team to play for, a job to do. His goal had always been to escape Wicksburg, not move back and marry a hometown girl.

Whoa. Where had that come from? Marriage had always been a four-letter word to him.

"The team's training staff is itching to work with you," Blake said. "They've been concerned about your training and conditioning."

"They'll be pleasantly surprised."

"Exactly what I hoped you'd say." Blake sounded like he was smiling. "My assistant can make your travel arrangements to Phoenix when you're ready."

Ryland's stomach knotted. He should be ready to leave now

after weeks in Wicksburg, but Phoenix didn't hold the same appeal for some reason. "I see the orthopedist this afternoon."

"I hope we hear good news."

We. The only "we" that had come to matter to Ryland was him and Lucy. Uh, Lucy and the Defeeters, that is. They were a package. Emotion tightened his throat. "I'll let you know."

Face it. What could he do? No matter how wonderful Lucy might be, Ryland wasn't picket-fence material, even if he could now understand the appeal of a committed, monogamous relationship. Marriage wasn't a goal of his. He had a career to salvage. The longer he stuck around playing at having a relationship, the deeper things would get and he might end up hurting Lucy.

Ryland knew what he had to do. Get the hell out of Wicksburg. And get out fast before he did any more damage than he'd already done.

CHAPTER TWELVE

OUT on the field Wednesday afternoon, Lucy glanced at her watch. Fifteen minutes until the end of today's practice. Strange. Ryland had yet to show up or call. She glanced at the parking lot, but didn't see his father's blue truck.

Even though he'd annoyed her on Monday night, she still wanted to see him. She hoped nothing was wrong. He'd bowed out of dinner last night. After Connor went to bed, she'd used the time to paint.

Marco passed the ball to Tyler. Connor, playing defense, stole the ball and kicked it out of bounds.

Lucy blew the whistle. "Push-ups for the entire team if the ball goes out again."

The boys groaned.

She scooped up the ball and tossed it onto the field. Play continued.

"You're doing great, coach."

Her toes curled at the sound of Ryland's voice. She glanced over her shoulder. He walked toward her in a T-shirt and shorts and…

She stared in shock at the tennis shoe on his right foot. "Your boot. It's gone."

"I no longer need it."

"That's great." And then she realized what that meant. With his foot healed, he would return to Phoenix. Her heart sank, but she kept a smile on her face. Pride kept her from showing how much he'd gotten to her. "I'm happy for you."

"Thanks." He stared at her with a strange look in his eyes. "I want to talk to the boys."

Her muscles tensed. Lucy had a feeling this might not be his usual end-of-practice pep talk. She blew the whistle.

The boys stopped playing and looked her way. Smiles erupted on their faces when they saw Ryland.

He motioned to them. "Everyone gather around."

The boys sat on the grass in front of Ryland. So did Lucy.

"Sorry I was late for practice, but I like what I saw out there," Ryland said. "Keep talking to each other, passing the ball and listening to your coach."

He winked at Lucy.

Her tight shoulder muscles relaxed a little.

"I appreciate how hard you're working. I know the drills we do can be boring, but they work. If you do them enough times at practice, you won't have to think about doing the moves in a game. It'll just happen."

"I can't wait until Saturday's match," Connor said.

"Me, either," Jacob agreed.

The other boys nodded.

Ryland dragged his hand through his hair. "I know you guys are going to play hard on Saturday. But I won't be there. My foot's better. It's time for me to return to my team."

Frowns met his words. Sighs, too. The disappointment on the boys' faces was clear. The kids talked over one another. A few were visibly shaken by the news.

Tears stung Lucy's eyes. She blinked them away. She needed to be strong for Connor and the team. "Let Ryland finish."

The boys quieted.

"I'm sorry I won't be able to be with you during those last two games," he said. "But Coach Lucy will do a great job."

She cleared her dry throat. "Why don't we thank Ryland for all his help with the team?"

The boys shouted the Defeeters' cheer, but the words lacked the same enthusiasm shown on game day. Their hearts weren't in it.

Lucy didn't blame them. Her heart was having a tough time,

too. She couldn't believe Ryland hadn't told her about leaving before he'd told the boys. He could have called if he hadn't had time. Even sent a text. But then she remembered the all-too-familiar words.

No promises. No guarantees.

Lucy couldn't be angry with him. Disappointed, yes. But Ryland hadn't played her. He hadn't lied. She'd known all along he was leaving. So did the boys and their parents. She just wasn't ready for the reality of it.

But this couldn't be goodbye. Even if he wasn't willing to admit it, they'd had too much fun, gotten to know each other too well for their dating to simply end. Of that, she was certain. They would stay in contact and see each other...somehow.

While Ryland said goodbye to each boy personally, she gathered up the equipment. As they finished, the boys ran off the field toward their parents.

Finally it was Connor's turn. He threw himself against Ryland and held on tight.

Her nephew's distress clogged Lucy's throat with emotion. She hoped this didn't put him back into a funk. He'd been handling his parents' deployment much better recently. Ryland might have been part of their lives for only a short time, but Connor had already gotten attached.

As Ryland spoke to her nephew, Connor wiped his eyes. This was one more difficult goodbye for the nine-year-old. But it wouldn't be a forever kind of goodbye. Ryland wouldn't do that to the kid, to his bud.

Someone touched Lucy's arm.

"Marco is in the car pouting. He told me Ryland is leaving," Suzy said. "I take it you didn't know."

"I knew he would be leaving. I just didn't know when," Lucy admitted.

"Cheryl showed me that article. His leaving won't change anything between you. You'll see each other. Every chance you can get."

Lucy nodded, hoping that was true.

"I'm going to take Marco to the pizza parlor for dinner. I'll take Connor with us," Suzy said. "You need some alone time with Ryland."

Yes, Lucy did. "I'll meet you there."

"If not, you can pick Connor up at my house."

She appreciated Suzy's thoughtfulness. "Thanks so much."

Suzy winked. "Don't do anything I wouldn't do."

Lucy could imagine what Suzy would want to do. If only she were that brave...

All Lucy could think about was how much she would miss Ryland, his company and his kisses. The memories would have to suffice until they saw each other again.

Ryland finished talking with Connor and sent him over to Lucy. She hugged her nephew and explained the plans for the evening.

Connor nodded, but the sadness in his eyes made her think he was simply going through the motions. Still, he hadn't said no. Being with Marco and having pizza, soda and video games might help Connor feel better.

Lucy watched Suzy walk off the field with an arm around Connor.

"He's upset," Ryland said, sounding almost surprised.

"He's had to say goodbye to his parents and now you," Lucy explained. "That's a lot for a nine-year-old boy to deal with."

"He'll rally."

Eventually. "So when are you leaving?"

"Tonight."

The air whooshed from her lungs. "That soon?"

"You knew I'd be leaving."

"Yes, I did." She kept her voice steady. Even though she was trembling inside, getting emotional would be bad. "But I thought I'd find out before everyone else."

She expected an apology or to hear him say this wasn't really goodbye because they would see each other soon.

"I have to go."

No apology. Okay. "You want to go."

A muscle twitched at his jaw. "Yeah, I do. I'm a soccer player. I want to play."

"I was thinking Connor and I could come and watch you play against the Rage when you come to Indianapolis."

"That would be—" Ryland dragged his hand through his hair "—not a good idea."

His words startled her. "Connor wants to see you play. So do I."

"I'm going to be busy."

"Too busy to say hello to us?"

"I need to focus on my career," Ryland said, his voice void of emotion. "I don't want a long-distance relationship or a girlfriend. I thought we were clear—"

"You can't tell me the time we spent together didn't mean anything to you." Hurt, raw and jagged, may have been ripping through her, but anger sounded in her voice. Lucy didn't care. She'd fallen in love with Ryland. She believed with her whole heart that he had feelings for her, too. "Or all those kisses."

"You know I like you," he said.

"Like." A far cry from love.

"Nothing more is possible."

Lucy stared down her nose. "Maybe not for you."

His gaze narrowed. "You said you weren't ready for a relationship or a boyfriend."

"I wasn't, but you showed me how good things could be. You opened me up to the possibility."

"I…" He stared at the grass. "I'm sorry, but I don't think something more between us would work out."

"It would." Her eyes didn't waver even though he wasn't looking at her. "I think you know it, too."

His gaze jerked up.

"You've admitted we're good together," she added.

"Chemistry."

"It's not just physical."

"We were never that physical."

"Sex is the easy part. Everything else is a lot harder."

"If we can't even manage the sex part, then we're not going to be able to handle anything else."

Ryland might like her. He might even care for her. But he

would downplay whatever he felt because it would be too hard for him to deal with. Distancing himself rather than admitting how he felt would be much easier. He liked being a famous foot-baller. Soccer was safe. What he'd found here in Wicksburg with her wasn't.

Lucy took a deep breath. "You're scared."

"I'm not scared of you," he denied.

"You're scared of yourself and your feelings because there might be something more important in your life than soccer."

"That's crazy."

"No, it's not." Sympathy washed over her. "I've felt the same way myself. Not wanting to take any risks so I wouldn't get hurt."

He shook his head. "Did you take some headers with the boys during practice?"

Lucy wasn't about to be distracted. She pursed her lips. "I know you. Better than you realize. I'm not deluding myself. I'm finally being honest with you. But it's too late."

"I know you're upset. I have time before my flight. I can drive you home."

"No." The force of the word stunned her as much as Ryland. She almost backed down, but realized she couldn't. Dragging this out any longer wouldn't be good for either one of them. It was obvious he was pushing her away. Ryland wasn't ready to step onto the pitch and take the kickoff from her. She'd thought he was different, but he wasn't. Not really.

If he couldn't be honest with himself, how could he ever be honest with her? Bottom line, he couldn't. Even though her heart was splintering into tiny pieces, she needed to let him go.

"It's time we said goodbye." She would make this easy on him. Lucy took a deep breath. "Thank you your help with the team and Connor. You've taught me a lot. More than I expected to learn. Good luck. I hope you have a great career and a very nice life."

His nostrils flared. "That's it?"

That was all he wanted to hear from her. He wasn't about to

say what she needed to hear. That he…cared. And even though she was positive he did, he couldn't say it.

Her heart pounded in her throat. Her lower lip quivered.

Hold it together. She didn't want him to see her break down. "Yeah, that's it."

Time to get out of here. Lucy gripped the equipment bag. She forced her feet to move across the field, but it wasn't easy. Her tennis shoes felt more like cement blocks. Each step took concentration. She wasn't sure she would make it all the way to her car.

Her insides trembled. Her hands shook. She thought nothing could match the heartache and betrayal of her husband and best friend. But the way she felt about Ryland…

I really do love him.

A sob wracked through her. Tears blurred her vision. She gripped the equipment bag until her knuckles turned white and her fingernails dug into her palms.

"Lucy," he called after her.

She forced her feet to keep walking.

Even though Lucy was tempted, she didn't look back. She couldn't. Not with the tears streaming down her face. And not when Ryland wasn't ready to admit the truth.

Saturday evening in Phoenix, Ryland stood next to the wall of floor-to-ceiling windows in his condominium. He rested his arm against the glass and stared at the city lights.

What a day.

He'd gotten an assist as an eighty-fourth minute substitute. He hadn't expected any playing time his first game back, but was happy contributing to the 2–1 win. Mr. McElroy had greeted Ryland with a handshake when he came off the pitch. Coach Fritz had said to expect more playing time during a friendly scheduled for Wednesday and next Saturday's game.

Ryland James was back in a big way. Blake agreed. His teammates, however, were more subdued about Ryland's return. A few handshakes, some glares.

He didn't blame them. He was captain of the team and had

missed the start of the season because he'd goofed off and injured himself. Really bad form. Irresponsible. Like much of
his behavior last season and the one before that. At practice,
he'd apologized, but it would take time to build that sense of
camaraderie. He was okay with that.

On the coffee table behind him, his cell phone beeped and
vibrated with each voice message and text that arrived. People,
including the bevy of beauties he'd left behind, were more than
happy to welcome him home with invitations to join them tonight at various clubs and parties, but he didn't feel like going
out and being social. Not when that scene meant nothing to
him now.

He kept thinking about Lucy and Connor and the rest of the
boys. The Defeeters had played a match today. Ryland wondered how they did. He hoped they'd played well.

A part of him was tempted to call and find out. But appeas-
ing his curiosity might only hurt Lucy more. She'd been angry
with him. Hurting her hadn't been his intent, but he'd done it
anyway and felt like a jerk.

Ryland missed Lucy, longed to see her, hear her voice, touch
her, kiss her. But he needed to leave her alone. He needed to
respect her decision to say goodbye the way she had. Respect
her.

Aaron had warned her not to see him. Rightfully so. She
deserved more than Ryland could give her. Not that he'd offered her anything. But he'd thought she was okay with that.
Instead, she'd gotten upset at him. Told him he was scared.

Yeah, right.

All he'd tried to do was be honest with her. That had worked
out real well.

Regret poked at Ryland. Maybe he could have done things
better. Told her about his leaving differently. Said more… He
shook it off.

What was he supposed to do? Give Lucy an engagement
ring as Blake had suggested? Pretend he felt more for her than
he did? She deserved better than that.

His cell phone rang. The ringtone told him it was his mother. "Hey, Mom. Did you watch the game?"

"No, we lost power."

Her voice sounded shaky. His shoulders tensed. "Is everything okay?"

"A tornado touched down near the elementary school. Your father and I are okay, so is the house, but we don't know the extent of the damage elsewhere," she said, her voice tight. "A tornado watch is still in effect. We're in the basement with Cupcake."

"Stay there. Keep me posted." Concern over Lucy and Connor overshadowed Ryland's relief at his parents being safe. A ball-size knot formed in his gut. "I love you, but I need to make a call right now."

"Lucy?"

"Yes."

"Let us know if she needs anything or a place to stay."

A potent mix of adrenaline and fear pulsed through him. He hit Lucy's cell-phone number on his contact list. Aaron's house was nowhere near the elementary school, but Ryland couldn't stop worrying. The Wicksburg soccer league played homes games at the elementary and middle schools. If the tornado touched down during match time…

There would have been sirens. No one would have been out at that point. Still he paced in front of the windows.

The phone rang.

Tornado warnings were all too common in the Midwest, especially in springtime. More than once he'd found himself in the bathroom of their apartment building in the tub with a mattress over him. But the twisters had always touched down on farmland, never in town.

On the fourth ring, Lucy's voice mail picked up. "I can't talk right now, but leave a message and I'll call you back."

The sound of her sweet voice twisted his insides. His chest hurt so badly he could barely breathe. He should be in Wicksburg, not here in Phoenix.

"Beep."

Ryland opened his mouth to speak, but no words came out. Not that he had a clue what he wanted to say if he could talk. He disconnected from the call.

Maybe she didn't have her cell phone with her. If she were at home...

He called the landline at Aaron's house. The phone rang. Again and again.

Ryland's frustration built so did his fear. He clenched his hand. Why wasn't she answering? Where could she be?

"Hello?" a young voice answered.

He clutched the back of the couch. His fingers dug into the buttery leather. "Connor?"

"Ryland." The relief in the boy's voice reached across the distance and squeezed Ryland's heart like a vise grip. "I knew you wouldn't forget about us."

"Never." The word came from somewhere deep inside him, spoken with a voice he didn't recognize. "My mom called me about the tornado."

"Aunt Lucy and I got inside the closet in the basement with pillows, a couple flashlights and the phone. It's one of those old dial ones." His voice trembled. "I have my DS, too."

"Extra playing time for you," Ryland teased, but his words fell flat. "Can I talk to your aunt?"

"She's looking for Manny."

The fat cat always tried to escape whenever the door opened. But if he'd gotten out today... "Where is he?"

"I don't know. Aunt Lucy moved the car into the garage and thinks he could have slipped out because she was in a hurry," Connor said. "We couldn't find him after the warning sounded. The siren might have scared him."

Sounded like Manny wasn't the only one frightened by the noise. Poor kid. "Your aunt will find him."

The alternative, for both Lucy and Manny, was unacceptable. Ryland glanced at the clock. If he caught a red-eye to Chicago and drove... But he had a team meeting tomorrow. And would Lucy want him to show up uninvited in the morning?

"Aunt Lucy said she would be back soon," Connor said finally. "She waited until the siren stopped to go outside. She didn't want to leave me alone if it wasn't safe."

Lucy would never put her nephew at risk, but Ryland didn't like the thought of her outside in that kind of weather with a tornado watch still in effect.

Silence filled the line.

"You hanging in there, bud?" he asked.

"Yeah," Connor said. "But the flashlight died. It's kind of dark."

Ryland grimaced. "See if your DS gives off some light."

"That helps a little."

Being thousands of miles away sucked. "I wish I were there."

"Me, too. But even if you were, you still wouldn't get to see our last game next Saturday," Connor said.

"Why not?"

"The field was destroyed so the season is over with. No more soccer until fall. If then."

"Because of the tornado?" Ryland asked.

"Yeah. Marco's mom called earlier," Connor explained. "My school is gone. The fields. The middle school. Some of the houses around there, too."

Gone. Stunned, Ryland tried to picture it. He couldn't. "Are Marco and his family, okay?"

"Yeah, but a tree landed on their car. Marco's dad is mad."

"Cars can be replaced." People couldn't.

Lucy.

Ryland wanted her in the basement with Connor, not out looking for Manny.

Damn. He hated not being able to do anything to help. Not that Lucy would want *his* help. Still… He gripped the phone.

Images of his weeks in Wicksburg flashed through his mind like a slideshow. Lucy handing him a container of cookies, teaching her how to do the warm-up routine and drills, watching her coach during the first match, drinking slushies with the team after games, kissing her.

You said you weren't ready for a relationship or a boyfriend. I wasn't, but you showed me how good things could be.

Things had been good. Great. If he could go back and do over his last day in Wicksburg…

But soccer had been the only thing on his mind. That and getting the hell out of town, running away as his mom had accused him of doing before.

A lump formed in his throat and burned like a flame.

"It's probably a good thing we can't play the last game." Connor's voice forced Ryland to focus on the present. "We got beat six–nothing today. Aunt Lucy said we were going through the motions and our hearts weren't in the game."

That was how Ryland had spent the last two years. He'd gotten tired of having to prove himself over and over again. He'd lost his hunger, his drive and his edge. He'd acted out without realizing it or the reasons behind his actions—anger, unhappiness and pressure. But he hadn't figured out how self-destructive his behavior had become until he'd returned to Wicksburg. Lucy and the boys had been his inspiration and let him rediscover the joy of the game. He'd connected with them in a way he hadn't since leaving town as a teenager.

And Lucy…

She showed him it wasn't about proving things to others, but to himself.

"The Strikers would have killed us anyway," Connor continued talking about the game that wouldn't be. He sounded more like himself, less scared. "Ten–nothing or worse."

Ryland may have gotten his soccer career back on track here, but he still had things to take care of in Wicksburg. He wasn't about to drop the ball again. "No way. The entire team has improved since that first match. The Strikers won by three goals. You need to play that game if only to prove you can challenge them."

"There's no field to play on."

"Come on." Ryland couldn't let those boys down after all they'd given him. He pictured each of their faces. In a short time, he'd learned their strengths and discovered their weaknesses. Secrets were hard to keep when you were nine and ten. He'd watched their skills improve, but also saw other changes like limbs lengthening and faces thinning. "That's not the Defeeter attitude."

"It was a big tornado."

And a big loss with the game today. Ryland took responsibility for that. The way he'd left, as if he could ride into town and then just leave again without anyone noticing or being affected was selfish and stupid. "No worries, bud. I'll figure something out."

"Really?"

"Really." Ryland didn't hesitate. He would find the team a place to play next Saturday. "Is your aunt back?"

"No, but I don't know how to use call-waiting. I should get off the phone in case she needs to talk to me."

"Smart thinking. Tell your aunt to call me when she finds Manny." Ryland checked the time again. "I'll let you know where you're going to play against the Strikers."

"I wish you could be there if we get to play."

"So do I." A weight pressed down on Ryland. "There's no place I'd rather be than with you and the team and your aunt Lucy."

But it wasn't possible. Ryland had an away match next Saturday. He was supposed to get playing time. But he needed to be in Wicksburg with Lucy and the boys.

Just remember, actions speak louder than words.

Blake's words echoed through Ryland's mind. He straightened. He'd been so blind. What he wanted—needed—was right there in front of him. Not here in Phoenix, but in Wicksburg. He just hadn't wanted to see it.

But now…

Time to stop talking about what he wanted and make it happen.

For the boys.

And most importantly, with Lucy.

CHAPTER THIRTEEN

Lucy's arms, scratched and sore after digging through tree limbs and debris to reach a howling Manny, struggled to carry the squirming, wet cat with a flashlight in her hand down to the basement. The warning siren remained silent, but they would sleep downstairs to be on the safe side. "You need to go on a diet, cat."

"Aunt Lucy?" Connor called from the closet. "Did you find Manny?"

"I found him." She opened the door, happy to see her nephew safe, dry and warm. "Why is it so dark in there?"

"The flashlight stopped working."

Yet Connor had stayed as she asked, even in the pitch-black when he had to be scared. Her heart swelled with pride and love for her nephew. Aaron and Dana were raising a great kid. "Sorry about that. The batteries must have been low."

"It's okay." He held up his glowing DS console. "I had a little light."

Manny pawed trying to get away from her. The cat looked like a drowned rat with his wet fur plastered against his body. "I think someone wants to see you."

Connor reached for the cat. "Where was he?"

"In the bushes across the street. I have a feeling he's had quite an adventure." Enough to last eight lives given the winds and flying debris the cat must have experienced. "I doubt he'll be so quick to dash outside again."

Connor cuddled Manny, who settled against her nephew's

chest as if that were his rightful and only place of rest. At least until a better spot came along. "Oh, Ryland called."

Lucy's heart jolted. She hadn't expected to hear from him again. "When?"

"A little while ago." Connor rubbed his chin against the cat. Manny purred like a V-8 engine. "He wants you to call him back. He was worried about you finding Manny."

Lucy whipped out her cell phone. Service had been spotty due to the storm, but three bars appeared. She went to press Ryland's number.

Wait. Her finger hovered over the screen. Calling him back would be stupid. Okay, it was nice he was concerned enough to call and want to know about Manny. But this went beyond what was happening in Wicksburg today.

Lucy had been thinking about him constantly since he left town. She missed him terribly. She needed to get him off her mind and out of her heart. But she wouldn't ignore his request completely. That would be rude.

Lucy typed in a text message and hit Send. Now she could go back to trying to forget about him.

Early Monday morning, Ryland stood in the reception area of the Phoenix Fuego headquarters. He'd spent much of yesterday trying to figure how to help those affected by the tornado in Wicksburg. Money was easy to donate. But he wanted to do something for the team and Lucy.

Waiting, he reread the text she'd sent him.

Manny wet & hungry but fine.

Ryland had wanted to hear her voice to know she was okay. He'd received a six-word text, instead. Probably more than he deserved.

The attractive, young personal assistant, who was always cheering on the team during games, motioned to the door to her right. "Mr. McElroy will see you now."

"Thanks." Ryland entered the owner's office. The plush furnishings didn't surprise him. All the photos of children everywhere did. "I appreciate you seeing me on such short notice."

Mr. McElroy shook his hand. "You said it was important."

"Yes."

He pointed to a leather chair. "Have a seat."

Ryland sat. "A tornado rolled through my hometown on Saturday night."

"I heard about that on the news. No casualties."

"No, but homes, two schools and several soccer fields in town were destroyed," Ryland said. "The Defeeters, a U-9 Boys rec. team I worked with while I was home, has their final game of the season this Saturday, but nowhere to play. I want to find them, and all the teams affected by the tornado, fields so they can finish out their spring season. I'd also like to be on the sideline with the Defeeters when they play."

Mr. McElroy studied him. "This sounds important to you."

"Yes," Ryland said. "I'm who I am today because of the start I got in that soccer league. I owe them and the Defeeters."

Not to mention Lucy. He wanted a second chance with her. A do over like young players sometimes received from refs when they made a bad throw-in or didn't quite get the ball over the line during kickoffs.

"That's thoughtful, but haven't you forgotten about the match against the Rage on Saturday night?"

Mr. McElroy's words echoed Blake's, but Ryland continued undeterred. "The Rage plays in Indianapolis. The stadium is a couple hours from Wicksburg. I know a way I can be at both games, but I'm going to need some help to pull it off. Your help, Mr. McElroy, and the owner of the Rage."

A tense silence enveloped the office. Ryland sat patiently waiting for the opportunity to say more.

"You've been nothing but a thorn in my side since I bought this team." Mr. McElroy leaned forward and rested his elbows on the desk. "Why should I help you?"

"Because it's the right thing to do."

"Right for the kids affected by the tornado?"

"And for us. Those kids are the future of soccer, both players and fans." Ryland spoke from his heart. The way Lucy would have wanted him to. "I know you don't want me on the team. I wasn't okay with that before. I am now. I don't care what team I'm on as long as I can play. But until the transfer window opens so you can loan me out across the pond, you need me as much as I need you."

Mr. McElroy's eyes widened. No doubt the truth had surprised him. "What kind of help are you talking about?"

Ryland explained his plan. "This is not only good for the players and the local soccer league, but it's also a smart PR move for the Fuego and Rage."

"Not smart. Brilliant. You can't buy that kind of publicity." Mr. McElroy studied him. "You're not the same player who left the club in March. What happened while you were away?"

"That U-9 team of boys taught me a few things about soccer I'd forgotten, and I met a girl who made me realize I'm more than just a footballer."

Smiling, Mr. McElroy leaned back in his chair. "You have my full support. I'll call the owner of the Rage this morning. Tell my assistant what you need to pull this off."

Satisfaction and relief loosened the knot in Ryland's gut. He stood. "Thank you, sir."

"I hope it all works out the way you planned," Mr. McElroy said.

"So do I."

Ryland had no doubt the soccer part would work, but he wasn't as confident about his plans for Lucy. He couldn't imagine his life without her.

She'd been right. Ryland had been scared. He still was. He just hoped it wasn't too late.

On Saturday, Lucy entered the training facility of the Indianapolis Rage. The MLS team had offered the use of their outdoor field for the final game of the Defeeters' spring soccer season against the Strikers.

Parents and players from both teams looked around in awe.

The training field resembled a ministadium complete with lights, two benches and bleachers.

Lucy couldn't believe they were here.

When the soccer league president had offered the Defeeters an all-expenses-paid trip to Indianapolis to play their final game of the season, she thought Ryland was behind it because Fuego was playing the Rage that same day. But then she learned all youth soccer teams without fields to finish the spring season had been invited.

She hadn't known whether to feel relieved or disappointed.

Pathetic. No matter how hard she tried to push Ryland out of her mind and heart, he was still there. She wondered how long he would remain there—days, weeks, months...

Stop thinking about him.

Connor ran onto the field, his feet encased in bright yellow soccer shoes. The other kids followed, jumping and laughing, as if the damage back home was nothing more than a bad dream.

"This is just what we all needed after the tornado." Suzy took a picture of the boys standing on the center mark of the field. "A weekend getaway and a chance to end the soccer season in style."

"The hotel is so nice." Cheryl's house had been damaged by the tornado. They were staying with Dalton's father, who had traveled with them for today's game. Maybe something good would come from all of this and they could work out their differences before the separation led to a divorce. "I can't wait for tonight. I've never been to a professional soccer game before."

Tickets to the Rage vs. Fuego match had been provided to each family. Much to the delight of the boys, who couldn't wait to see Ryland play. Connor was beside himself with excitement, positive his favorite player would be in the game for the entire ninety minutes.

Lucy hoped not. Watching Ryland play for only few minutes would be difficult let alone the entire match. Hearing his name mentioned hurt. Connor talked constantly about Ryland. That made it hard to forget him.

Thing would get better. Eventually. She'd been in this same

place before with Jeff. Except with Ryland the hurt cut deeper. Her marriage had never been a true partnership, but she'd felt that way with Ryland, in spite of the short time they'd been together.

She shook off the thought. The match will be a nice way to cap off the day.

The boys screamed, the noise deafening. Only one thing—one person—could elicit that kind of response.

Her throat tightened.

Ryland was here.

Emotions churned inside her.

"That man gets hotter each time I see him." Cheryl whistled. "But who are all his buddies?"

"Yowza," Suzy said. "If it gets any hotter in here, I think I'm going to need to fan myself."

"Am I a bad mom if I'm jealous of a bunch of eight- and nine-year-olds?" Debbie asked.

"I hope not, because I feel the same way," Cheryl replied.

Lucy kept her back turned so she wouldn't be tempted to look at Ryland. But the women had piqued her curiosity. "What are you talking about?"

"Turn around." Cheryl winked. "Trust me, you won't be disappointed."

Reluctantly, Lucy turned. She stared in disbelief. Nearly a dozen professional soccer players with killer bodies and smiling faces worked with the Defeeters and the Strikers, helping the boys warm-up and giving them pointers.

One Fuego player, however, stood out from all the others. *Ryland.*

His dark hair was neatly combed, his face clean shaven. He looked handsome in his Fuego uniform—blue, orange and white with red flames. But it was the man, not the athlete, who had stolen her heart. A weight pressed down on her chest, squeezing out what air remained in her lungs.

Suzy sent her a sympathetic smile. "This is a dream come true for the boys."

Cheryl nodded. "I think I've died and gone to heaven myself."

Lucy had gone straight to hell. Hurt splintered her already-aching heart. She struggled to breathe. She didn't even attempt to speak.

Everyone around her smiled and laughed. She wanted to cry. If only he could see how good the two of them would be together...

"Look at all the photographers and news crews," Suzy said.

Cheryl combed through her hair and pinched her cheeks. "No wonder the league had us sign those photo releases."

The media descended on the field, but their presence didn't distract the professional players from the kids. The boys, however, mugged for the cameras.

As the warm-up period drew to an end, the referee called over the Strikers. That was Lucy's cue to get ready. She had player cards to show the ref and her clipboard with the starting lineup and substitution schedule so each boy would play an equal amount of time.

"We're taping the game." Debbie motioned to the bleachers where her husband adjusted a tripod. "For Aaron and Dana."

"Thanks," Lucy said.

The referee called the Defeeters over.

Nerves threatened to get the best of Lucy. But in spite of all the hoopla and media, this was still a rec. soccer game. She had no reason to interact with Ryland and wouldn't.

With her resolve in place, Lucy lined up the boys for the ref. Ryland stood near the Defeeters' bench.

Her heart rate careened out of control.

Oh, no. He was planning to be there during the match.

The ref excused the Defeeters. As she walked to the bench, she looked everywhere, but at Ryland. Maybe if she didn't catch his eye or say—

"It's good to see you, Lucy," he said.

Darn. She cleared her dry throat. "The boys are so happy you're here."

"This is the only place I want to be."

The referee blew his whistle, saving her from having to speak with him.

The game was fast-paced with lots of action and scoring. At halftime with the score Defeeters two and Strikers three, Ryland talked to the boys about the game. With two minutes remaining in regulation time, Connor stole the ball from a defender and broke away up the left sideline. He crossed the ball in front of the goal. Dalton kicked the ball into the corner of the net.

Tie score!

The parents screamed. The boys gave each other high fives.

The Strikers pulled their goalie. A risky move, but they wanted an extra player in the game. The offense hit hard after the kickoff, took a shot on goal, but missed.

Defeeters' turn. Marco took the ball. His pass to Dalton was stolen. The Strikers' forward headed down the field, but Connor sprinted to steal the ball. He kicked the ball down the line to Dalton, who passed it to Marco. The goal was right in front of him. All he had to do was shoot at the empty goal.

"Shoot," Ryland yelled. So did everyone else.

The referee blew his whistle. The game was over.

The Defeeters had tied the Strikers.

"Great job, coach," Ryland said to her. "You've come a long way."

But she had so much further to go, especially when it came to getting over him. She didn't smile or look at him. "Thanks."

"You boys played a great game," Ryland said to the excited boys gathered around him. "The best all season."

Lucy knew they would rather hear from him than her. She didn't mind that one bit.

Connor beamed. "You said we could challenge them. We did."

Ryland messed up the kid's hair. "You did more than that, bud."

The two teams lined up with the coaches at the end, followed by the professional players, and shook hands. Ryland and the other players passed out T-shirts to both teams, posed for pictures and signed autographs. Talk about a dream come true. And there was still the match to attend tonight.

She gathered up the balls and equipment. "Come on, Connor. We can go back to the hotel for a swim before the game."

Connor looked at Ryland then back at her.

Lucy's heart lodged in her throat. She knew that conspiratorial look of his.

"I'm riding back to the hotel with Marco and his family," Connor said.

"I told the boys we could stop for an after-game treat on the way back to the hotel," Suzy said.

"Slushies, slushies," the boys chanted.

Those had become the new Defeeter tradition. Thanks to Ryland. But he wasn't offering to take the team out today.

Lucy remembered. He had to prepare for the match against the Rage tonight.

She thought about offering to drive the boys herself, but from the look on Connor's face, he had his heart set on going with Marco. She couldn't ruin this magical day for him on the off chance Ryland might try to talk to her.

Time to act like an adult rather than a brokenhearted teenager. She raised her chin. "Sounds like fun. I'll meet you back at the hotel."

As the boys headed out, she followed them, eager to escape before Ryland—

"Lucy."

She kept walking, eyeing the exit.

"Please wait," Ryland said.

She stopped. Not because she wanted to talk to him, but because he'd helped her with the team. Five minutes. That was all the time he could have.

Ryland caught up to her. "You've been working hard with the boys."

"It's them, not me." She glanced back at the field. "I don't know what your part in making this happen was, but thank you. It meant a lot to the boys on both teams." She tried to sound nonchalant, but wasn't sure she was succeeding.

"I didn't do this only for them."

Her pulse accelerated.

"I'm sorry." His words came out in a rush. "The way I left was selfish. I was only thinking about myself. Not the boys. Definitely not you. I never meant to hurt anyone, but I did. I hope you can forgive me."

The sincerity in his eyes and voice tugged at her heart. She had to keep her heart immune. She had to get away from him. "You're forgiven."

His relief was palpable. "Thank you. You don't know what that means to me."

She didn't want to know. Just being this close to him was enough to make her want to bolt. The scent of him surrounded her. She wanted to bottle some up to take home with her. *Not a good idea.* "I need to get back to the hotel. Connor..."

Ryland took a step closer to her. "He's stopping for a snack on the way back."

Lucy stepped back. "I still should—"

"Stay."

The one word was a plea and a promise, full of anxiety and anticipation. She tried not to let that matter, but it wasn't easy. "Why?"

"There's more I want to say to you."

She glanced around the stadium. Everyone seemed to have left. "Make it quick."

He took a deep breath. "Soccer has been the only thing in my life for so long. I defined myself as a footballer. Playing made me feel worthy. But I lost the love for the game. The past couple of years, I made some bad decisions. I had no idea why I was acting out so badly until I got to Wicksburg. I realized how unhappy I'd been trying to keep proving myself with a new league, team and fans. Nothing satisfied me anymore. Working with the boys helped me discover what was missing. Soccer isn't only about scoring goals. I'd forgotten the value of teamwork. You made me realize I don't want soccer to be the only thing in my life. I want—I need—more than that. I need you, Lucy."

The wind whooshed from her lungs. She couldn't believe what he was saying.

"I know how important honesty is to you," he continued. "When I got to Phoenix, I realized you were right. I was scared. A coward. I wasn't being honest about my feelings. Not to you or myself. You mean so much to me. I'm finally able to admit it."

"I'm...touched. Really. But even if you're serious—"

"I am serious, Lucy." He took her hand in his. "More serious than I've ever been in my entire life. I was trapped by the expectations of others, the pressure, but you set me free. I'm more than just a soccer player. I don't want to lose you."

They way he looked at her, his gaze caressing her skin like a touch, brought tears to her eyes. She blinked them away. She couldn't lose sight of the truth.

Lucy took a deep breath. "We live in different worlds, different states. It would never work."

"I want to make it work."

"You know what happened with Jeff."

He nodded.

"Look at you," she said. "You're hot, wealthy, a superstar. Women want you. They fantasize about you. That's hard for me to handle."

"I know you've had some tough times in your life. We can't wash away everything that's happened before, but we can't dwell on it, either," he said. "Trust doesn't just happen. I can tell you all the right words you want to hear. That I'm not like Jeff. That I won't cheat. But what it really takes is a leap of faith. Are you willing to take that leap with me?"

Her heart screamed the answer it wanted her to say. Could she leap when her heart had been broken after spending only a few weeks with him? How could she not when Ryland was everything she'd dreamed about?

"When I was sick, people lied to me. The doctors, my parents, even Aaron. Maybe not outright lies, but untruths about the treatments, how I would feel and what I could do. I hated having to rely on people who couldn't be honest with me."

"So that's where your independent streak came from."

She nodded. "And then Jeff came along. He was honest with me, sometimes brutally so, but I liked that better than the alternative. I fell hard and fast only to find out he was nothing more than a lying, cheating jerk." She took a deep breath so she could keep going. "You've taught me so much and not only about soccer. Because of you I've learned I can accept help without feeling like a burden to someone. I've also learned I can forgive and trust again. I would love to take that leap with you. But I'm not sure I'm ready yet."

"I don't care how long it takes," he said. "I'll wait until you're ready."

"You're serious."

"Very." He kissed each of her fingers, sending pleasurable shivers up her arm. "I love you."

The air rushed from her lungs. She tried to speak, to question him, but couldn't.

Sincerity shone in his eyes. "I tried to pretend I didn't love you, but I'm no good at pretending when it comes to you."

Joy exploded inside her. She could tell they weren't just words. He meant them. Maybe taking the leap wouldn't be so hard. "I love you, too."

"That's the first step to taking the leap."

"Maybe the first two steps." Lucy kissed Ryland, a kiss full of hope and love and possibility. None of her dreams had come true so far, but maybe some...could.

Ryland pulled her against him. She went willingly, wrapping her arms around him. Her hand hit something tucked into the waistband of his shorts. It fell to the ground. She backed away.

A small blue box tied with a white ribbon lay on its side. She recognized the packaging from ads and the movies. The box was from Tiffany & Co.

Her mouth gaped. She closed it. He really was serious.

His cheeks reddened. "If I told you that's where I keep my lucky penny, I'm guessing you won't believe me."

Shock rendered her speechless.

"It's nothing." He took a breath. "Okay, I'll be honest. It's something, but it can wait. You're not ready right now."

She placed her hand on his. "Maybe I'm more ready than I realized."

As he handed her the box, hope filled his eyes. "This is for you. Today. A year from now. Whenever you're ready."

Lucy untied the ribbon and removed the top of the box. Inside was a midnight blue, almost black, suede ring box. Her hand trembled so much she couldn't get the smaller box out. She looked up at him.

"Allow me." Ryland pulled out the ring box and opened it. A Tiffany-cut diamond engagement ring sparkled against the dark navy fabric. The words Tiffany & Co. were embossed in gold foil on the lid. "Nothing matters except being with you. I love you. I want to marry you, Lucy, if you'll have me."

She couldn't believe this was happening. She forced herself to breathe. All her girlhood fantasies didn't compare to the reality of this moment. Ryland James had asked her to marry him. He'd been honest to himself and to her. He was fully committed to making it work. Lucy's heart and her mind agreed on the answer. Make the leap? She had no doubt at all. "Yes."

He placed the ring on her finger. A perfect fit, the way they were a perfect fit together. "There's no rush."

"No, there isn't." The love shining in his eyes matched her own. "Aaron and Dana won't be home until next year."

"It might take me that long to convince your brother I'm good enough for you."

"Probably," Lucy teased. "But with Connor in your corner, it might take only six months."

"Very funny."

She stared at the ring. A feeling of peace coursed through her. "So this officially makes me a WAG."

Ryland brushed his lips across hers. "A *G* who will eventually become a *W*. But you're already an *M*."

"An *M*?" Lucy asked.

"Mine."

"I'll always be your *M*. As long as you're mine, too."

"Always," he said. "I think I may have always been yours without even realizing it."

"If you're trying to score…"

"No need. I already won." Ryland pulled her against him and kissed her again. "I love you, Lucy."

A warm glow flowed through her, making her heart sigh. "I love you."

* * * * *

Mills & Boon® Hardback
June 2012

ROMANCE

A Secret Disgrace	Penny Jordan
The Dark Side of Desire	Julia James
The Forbidden Ferrara	Sarah Morgan
The Truth Behind his Touch	Cathy Williams
Enemies at the Altar	Melanie Milburne
A World She Doesn't Belong To	Natasha Tate
In Defiance of Duty	Caitlin Crews
In the Italian's Sights	Helen Brooks
Dare She Kiss & Tell?	Aimee Carson
Waking Up In The Wrong Bed	Natalie Anderson
Plain Jane in the Spotlight	Lucy Gordon
Battle for the Soldier's Heart	Cara Colter
It Started with a Crush...	Melissa McClone
The Navy Seal's Bride	Soraya Lane
My Greek Island Fling	Nina Harrington
A Girl Less Ordinary	Leah Ashton
Sydney Harbour Hospital: Bella's Wishlist	Emily Forbes
Celebrity in Braxton Falls	Judy Campbell

HISTORICAL

The Duchess Hunt	Elizabeth Beacon
Marriage of Mercy	Carla Kelly
Chained to the Barbarian	Carol Townend
My Fair Concubine	Jeannie Lin

MEDICAL

Doctor's Mile-High Fling	Tina Beckett
Hers For One Night Only?	Carol Marinelli
Unlocking the Surgeon's Heart	Jessica Matthews
Marriage Miracle in Swallowbrook	Abigail Gordon

0512 GEN STD HB

ROMANCE

An Offer She Can't Refuse	Emma Darcy
An Indecent Proposition	Carol Marinelli
A Night of Living Dangerously	Jennie Lucas
A Devilishly Dark Deal	Maggie Cox
The Cop, the Puppy and Me	Cara Colter
Back in the Soldier's Arms	Soraya Lane
Miss Prim and the Billionaire	Lucy Gordon
Dancing with Danger	Fiona Harper

HISTORICAL

The Disappearing Duchess	Anne Herries
Improper Miss Darling	Gail Whitiker
Beauty and the Scarred Hero	Emily May
Butterfly Swords	Jeannie Lin

MEDICAL

New Doc in Town	Meredith Webber
Orphan Under the Christmas Tree	Meredith Webber
The Night Before Christmas	Alison Roberts
Once a Good Girl...	Wendy S. Marcus
Surgeon in a Wedding Dress	Sue MacKay
The Boy Who Made Them Love Again	Scarlet Wilson

0512 GEN STD LP

Mills & Boon® Hardback

July 2012

ROMANCE

The Secrets She Carried	Lynne Graham
To Love, Honour and Betray	Jennie Lucas
Heart of a Desert Warrior	Lucy Monroe
Unnoticed and Untouched	Lynn Raye Harris
A Royal World Apart	Maisey Yates
Distracted by her Virtue	Maggie Cox
The Count's Prize	Christina Hollis
The Tarnished Jewel of Jazaar	Susanna Carr
Keeping Her Up All Night	Anna Cleary
The Rules of Engagement	Ally Blake
Argentinian in the Outback	Margaret Way
The Sheriff's Doorstep Baby	Teresa Carpenter
The Sheikh's Jewel	Melissa James
The Rebel Rancher	Donna Alward
Always the Best Man	Fiona Harper
How the Playboy Got Serious	Shirley Jump
Sydney Harbour Hospital: Marco's Temptation	Fiona McArthur
Dr Tall, Dark...and Dangerous?	Lynne Marshall

MEDICAL

The Legendary Playboy Surgeon	Alison Roberts
Falling for Her Impossible Boss	Alison Roberts
Letting Go With Dr Rodriguez	Fiona Lowe
Waking Up With His Runaway Bride	Louisa George

Mills & Boon® Large Print

July 2012

ROMANCE

Roccanti's Marriage Revenge	Lynne Graham
The Devil and Miss Jones	Kate Walker
Sheikh Without a Heart	Sandra Marton
Savas's Wildcat	Anne McAllister
A Bride for the Island Prince	Rebecca Winters
The Nanny and the Boss's Twins	Barbara McMahon
Once a Cowboy...	Patricia Thayer
When Chocolate Is Not Enough...	Nina Harrington

HISTORICAL

The Mysterious Lord Marlowe	Anne Herries
Marrying the Royal Marine	Carla Kelly
A Most Unladylike Adventure	Elizabeth Beacon
Seduced by Her Highland Warrior	Michelle Willingham

MEDICAL

The Boss She Can't Resist	Lucy Clark
Heart Surgeon, Hero...Husband?	Susan Carlisle
Dr Langley: Protector or Playboy?	Joanna Neil
Daredevil and Dr Kate	Leah Martyn
Spring Proposal in Swallowbrook	Abigail Gordon
Doctor's Guide to Dating in the Jungle	Tina Beckett

0612 GEN STD LP